Stations of Madness

Radar DeBoard

Book Cover by Grim Poppy Design

Edited by Tasha Reynolds

Interior formatting by Cat Voleur

First edition 2024

Contents

Prologue

An Unworthy Seeker

The disheveled man stumbled through his apartment, hands covering his ears to desperately drown out the unwanted sound. His efforts were in vain as the monotone and methodical voice continued to drone on. In a sudden cry of fury, he raced over to the speaker that was broadcasting the voice throughout his residence. He grabbed the device and threw it against the floor with all his might. There was minimal damage to the speaker, and it remained intact enough to continue working. Wasting no time, the man delivered a series of rage-filled stomps that shattered the device into dozens of pieces.

"I did it," the apartment's occupant whispered to himself as silence filled the room. "I stopped it."

Mere moments passed before the voice suddenly picked back up, filling the man with dread. He frantically ran about the room smashing all the electronic devices in his path as he desperately searched for the new source of the voice. After several minutes without any success, a realization dawned on him; he was hearing it inside his head. Somehow, his brain was directly receiving the broadcast, which happened to be the last thing he wanted.

"No! No! No!" he screamed at the ceiling of his apartment as he began beating the sides of his head. "I don't want this anymore. Stop this! Stop this!"

Despite his protests, the voice continued without pause. His brain became overwhelmed by the message being transmitted as pain welled up inside his head. Quickly, his mind headed toward the edge of oblivion, to the point where he could feel his sanity slipping away. The whole ordeal was too much to handle, and it soon became clear to the tenant that there was only one way out. Without a second thought, he charged toward the window overlooking the street in front of the apartment complex. He gained momentum rapidly, and when he was only a few feet from his goal, he leapt with all his might.

The full weight of his body was far more than the glass could hold and it easily shattered. He continued forward through the air for another foot or two after impact with the window, then began to plummet to the ground below. Being located on the third floor meant that his fall didn't take long, but it lasted long enough for him to realize the mistake he had just made. He let out a shriek of horror as he plummeted to his fate, but it was almost immediately silenced by him hitting the pavement with a sickening smack. The impact tore through skin and broke bones, splattering different parts of the man across the sidewalk. There were but a few people on the street unfortunate enough to witness the ordeal, but the shrieks of terror more than made up for their small numbers.

As a crowd began to form below, back inside the man's apartment, a presence watched the chaos unfolding. It seemed the mysterious entity had overestimated the constitution of the individual splattered across the street. The man did not have the mental fortitude to receive the full message and do what was needed of him. Though it was unfortunate, the outcome didn't really hinder the presence's progress. There were many more people in the world who would openly seek the message being sent. The vast majority of them would fail, just as the man had, but there would be a few who would succeed. All the presence had to do was wait for the next person to find the signal, and then see how long they lasted, just as it had done so many times before.

Part 1

First Transmissions

The dial slowly turned, causing the screeching static to change with it. Matt let out a deep sigh as he painstakingly tried to tune the radio. After another full turn of the dial, he sat back in his chair and rubbed his hands against his face. An overwhelming feeling of frustration bubbled up inside of him. Matt shot his hand through the air to slam it down against his desk, but he managed to stop himself at the last second. Instead, he slowly lowered his head and groaned.

"What the hell are you doing, Sampson?" Courtland asked as he entered the room.

Matt lifted his head off the desk and sighed, "I'm trying to find a number station."

"A number station? Freaking nerd, I didn't know you liked math that much," Court joked as he made his way over to Matt's desk. He looked between the open laptop and the giant radio that took up most of the space, leaving barely any room for Matt to rest his arms.

"From that response, I take it you've never heard of them before," Matt said as he glanced up at his roommate.

Court laughed. "No, I've never heard of a number station." He leaned down toward Matt. "You wanna know why?" Court whispered, "I'm not a loser."

Matt gently shoved Court. "Screw you, man."

Court clapped his hands together as he chuckled for a few seconds. He finally calmed down enough to ask, "So really, what is it?"

"It's a strange type of broadcast," Matt began to explain. "They've been around since radios have existed." He took another try at tuning the device but gave up when he didn't get anything immediately. "Anyway," he continued as he turned back toward Court, "there's supposedly dozens of these things all over the world, and all they ever do is just read off numbers."

"That's it?" Court skeptically responded. "Someone just rattles off a few numbers...and then what?"

"It's not just a few numbers," Matt said with a hint of excitement in his voice, "It's hundreds...no, thousands of numbers. Whoever reads them off, they spend several hours doing nothing but that."

"So some weirdo in his basement just reads off numbers...and you wanna listen to that?" Court condescendingly asked.

"It's not just one person," Matt quickly responded in a defensive tone, "There are dozens of people who are doing this."

"How do you know it's different people?" Court wondered. "You haven't heard them before, right?"

"I haven't," Matt replied, "but others have." He got on his laptop and pulled up an article he had been reading a few hours earlier. Matt read out, "There are dozens of number stations spread throughout the world. English is the primary language used by most of the stations, however, Greek, Russian, Italian, French, Mandarin Chinese, Japanese, and Spanish have also been utilized." He turned to Court, "See? It's a group of people who do this. There's no way one person could read something off in that many languages."

"Okay," Court said slowly, "I guess I just don't understand the appeal."

Matt raised an eyebrow. "What do you mean?"

"I don't get why anyone would want to listen to someone rattle off a bunch of random numbers in Russian." Court shook his head, "What's the point?"

Matt shrugged. "Nobody knows. These stations have existed for decades, but no one can figure out what the numbers are for." Matt stood up out of his office chair and stretched. "It's an absolute mystery. That's where the appeal comes in."

Court smiled. "I get it now. You're after a good mystery." He chuckled, "You're just trying to get some fame and fortune so you don't have to do a grad paper for Professor Burrows."

Matt shrugged, "I wouldn't mind getting out of doing that." He let out a heavy sigh. "A hundred pages is not something I'm looking forward to writing." Matt sat back down and gestured to the radio, "This helps take my mind off of it."

"Matt...this is exactly why man made video games," Court joked. "So you don't have to fiddle with this junk to have a good time anymore." He walked over to the entry-way and slipped his shoes on. Court turned back toward Matt with a sly smile. "Hey bud, I got something that will really take your mind off the paper."

"Oh really?" Matt skeptically replied, "And what's that?"

"You can double date with me tonight!" Court spat out.

"Absolutely not!" Matt exclaimed waving his arms. He glared at Court, "You know it's not really a double date if you leave after twenty minutes for a quick hump and dump."

"Oh come on!" Court protested. "You know I ain't like that." He pointed at Matt, "Name one time."

"Sonya," Matt spat out immediately. He grinned, "Of course, I could always go for a classic and say...Tiffany."

"Woah!" Court exclaimed, "We agreed that Tiffany doesn't count. That was just a bad situation that I walked into."

"Sure it was," Matt playfully responded, "I'm sure Sonya was too."

Court sighed, "Okay, you got me with that one." He walked toward Matt, "But you have to believe me, I'm actually wanting to date right now. I found a great girl and I'm just a little nervous is all." He dropped down to his knees. "I'm begging you, man! You gotta help me out."

"No can do," Matt said as he turned back to face his setup.

"Why not?" Court whined as he stood up. "I'm sure Madison would love it. You haven't taken her out in a while." He leaned in close to Matt, "This is your chance to treat her right for an evening. We're talking about some serious brownie points here, my man."

Matt looked at Court and chuckled, "The reason I haven't done anything romantic with Madison in a while is because she's been cramming for her midterms. I'm taking her out next week to celebrate finishing them all." He patted Court on the shoulder, "Nice try bud, but it looks like you're on your own tonight."

Court groaned, "Fine, you traitor." He fake-stomped over to the door, "I hope you have fun with your dumb numbers!"

"Good luck on the date!" Matt hollered.

"Thanks, bro!" Court shouted back as he opened and quickly closed the door behind him.

Matt took in a deep breath before focusing back in on his radio. He slowly turned the adjustment dial while listening for any tiny changes in the static. It didn't take long for his patience to wear thin, and he slammed his back against his chair. Matt grunted in frustration and sat there for a moment while the sound of constant static droned on. He decided now would be a good time to make something for dinner. Matt slowly stood up out of his chair and started to make his way to the kitchen.

As he did, a low, male voice just barely cut through the static. "Seven, forty-two."

Matt turned his head back toward his radio in astonishment. He wasn't tuning the frequency, and yet, the static was diminishing. With his curiosity peaked, he moved back to his desk and sat down. He frantically opened a new document on his computer and began to type out the numbers being spoken. As he was inputting the fifth number, he felt a slight ringing sensation in his ears that was accompanied by a hint of dizziness. He shook his head to try to get rid of the feeling as he kept typing. Only a few more seconds passed before the ringing rapidly increased in intensity. Suddenly, Matt didn't feel like moving anymore. His fingers started to slow down as his thoughts began to leave his mind. He couldn't do anything except sit there and listen to the numbers.

The feeling of someone shaking his shoulder brought Matt out of his trance. He blinked and noticed he was staring directly at a completely black computer screen. Slowly, he looked over his shoulder to see Court giving him a puzzled look.

"Hey." Matt drowsily asked, "How did the date go?"

"It um...it went pretty well," Court replied quietly. "Are you feeling okay man?" he asked with concern.

"Y-yeah, why?" Matt stammered.

"Because I came home and found you just sitting here."

"Well, I was listening to the numbers."

"No...you weren't." Court calmly disagreed before slowly recounting, "I came in and found you sitting completely still while your radio was blaring static."

"So the numbers weren't going?" Matt asked.

Court shook his head, "No, it was just static. You were staring at a blank screen while listening to static."

Matt could feel his roommate's anxious gaze looking at him. He didn't want his cohort to be worried about him, so he quickly tried to think of something to quell Court's concern. "I must have dozed off is all," Matt groggily answered. His response was as much for himself as it was for Court. "I had been listening to stuff for a while and just fell asleep."

"You fell asleep while sitting up...with your eyes open?" Court asked skeptically.

"Yup," Matt said quickly, standing up. "I use to do that all the time when I was a kid. I would fall asleep with my eyes open."

"Really?" Court said with surprise. He blinked a few times as he processed the new information, "Why didn't you ever tell me that?"

"It never got brought up," Matt shrugged. "Granted, I don't think that sort of thing comes up in normal conversation."

Court stared at Matt for a moment before shrugging. "Fair enough," he yawned. "Well, it's two in the morning so I'm gonna hit the hay." He started walking toward his room but turned back to Matt, "If you're gonna start doing this on a regular basis...please get some headphones."

"O-Of course," Matt hollered as he watched Court walk into his room and close the door. He slowly sunk back into his office chair and shook his head. It felt weird to him that he didn't remember falling asleep. In fact, besides the memory loss, he also didn't feel like his normal self at the current moment. Something was off, but he couldn't quite put a finger on what it was.

He sighed as he turned back to his desk, where he powered off the radio and then unlocked his computer. The first thing that he noticed on the screen was his open document with the numbers eleven and nineteen typed in it. Matt chuckled to himself as he closed the file without saving it. He must have been really tired since he only managed to write down two numbers before losing consciousness.

Matt entered his bedroom and hopped into bed. He pulled the blanket up to his neck and wriggled around until he got more comfortable. In the darkness, he couldn't help but look up at the ceiling and think about earlier in the night. He knew he heard someone reciting numbers, but he couldn't remember the voice or what they had said. After several minutes of trying to recall what had happened, he finally decided to let it go and get some sleep. He closed his eyes and waited to drift off. His mind, however, had different plans as it constantly wandered between thoughts of his classes and his love life with Madison. Eventually, his brain quieted down and he started to drift off. As he drew toward unconsciousness, a low, male voice sounded through his mind. The number seven, the first number that had heard, rang through his brain as he drifted off to sleep.

"You're still asleep?" Matt heard a voice shout.

He slowly opened his eyes and looked toward his door to see Court standing there. "What?" he muttered in confusion.

"You missed class," Court said folding his arms.

"I did?" Matt exclaimed in confusion as he sat up. "But I set my alarm for eight. How did this happen?"

"Because you slept through it," Court sarcastically replied. He sighed, "I expected you to miss the class after last night, but I didn't think I'd find you still asleep by the time I got back."

Matt rubbed his eyes as he asked, "What time is it?"

"It's twelve, dude," Court shook his head. "Even when we go binge drinking, you're awake by ten." He took a step into Matt's room, "Are you sure there's nothing wrong?"

"I'm fine," Matt insisted, "I just had a tough time getting to sleep, that's all." He stood up and stretched, "There were a couple of bad dreams that kept waking me up."

"What dreams?"

Matt shrugged, "I don't remember. I think it might have had something to do with that movie we watched a few nights ago."

"Night Gutter?" Court answered in skepticism. "That's a crappy B movie man. We made fun of it."

"I know, I know," Matt sighed, "I guess...all I can say is that the mind has a weird way of twisting things around when you're asleep." He walked up to Court and gestured for him to get out of the way. "I gotta piss bro."

Court sighed and moved aside. He stood at the doorway to Matt's room for a moment until his roommate had made it into the bathroom. Court took a few steps into the hall and shouted, "I'm gonna go get some lunch from the cafeteria. You wanna come with?"

"Nah," Matt replied through the door, "I'm not hungry."

Court sighed, "All right, I'll see you later tonight."

Matt finished his business and walked out of the bathroom to find that Court was already gone. He shuffled into the living room and stared at the sun slightly peeking through the curtains. With a loud sigh, he made his way over to his desk and plopped down. Matt rubbed his eyes again in an attempt to get rid of some of his drowsiness. He then turned on his computer and impatiently waited for the login screen to pop up. After typing in his password, he prepared himself for the task at hand. He brought up all the different articles he had been using for research and prepared to start writing.

Once he had cracked several of his knuckles, he got to work. For the first few sentences he had some real momentum going, though as soon as he reached the second paragraph, Matt started to slow down. By the time he had made it to the third paragraph, he was drawing a blank on what to write. He lightly pushed his chair back from the desk as he tried to brainstorm what to put next. The sudden sound of static took him by surprise, and he looked to see that his radio had somehow turned itself on.

A soft, female voice came through the static in a near whisper, "Sieben, zweiundvierzig."

"What the hell?" Matt muttered to himself as he turned off the radio.

He sat back in his chair and wondered what had caused it to turn on. His mind quickly pivoted to the numbers that had been read. It had been a long time since Matt had taken German, but he still knew enough to know that sieben was seven. He thought back to the previous night and tried to remember if the voice from then had also said seven. The harder he tried to remember, the more a pain started to grow in the middle of his forehead. Eventually, he stopped and decided to focus on his paper.

Matt concentrated his efforts for several hours on making it somewhere with his gargantuan assignment. After stopping a few times to look at funny videos online, he managed to get about six pages typed up. As he tried to start in on the first sentence on the seventh page, he let out a groan of exhaustion and stared at his computer screen. Even though he had only woken up a few hours ago, he was already feeling drained. Then again, that always happened when he was forced to write something. Nothing was more taxing on his mind than typing up a paper for a class.

"I guess it's dinner time," Matt sighed, looking at his phone.

He stood up from his desk and made his way over to the kitchen. As he was rummaging around in the fridge, the noise of static started to fill the apartment. Matt brought a handful of different lunchmeats out and set them down on the counter. He finally noticed the out-of-place noise as he was going for some bread. Matt stared across the apartment at the device in confusion. There was no way he turned it on, which only left one possibility as to why he was hearing static, the radio must have somehow done it. A shiver ran down his spine as he mulled over that idea. Taking in a deep breath, he took a few tentative steps out of the kitchen toward his desk.

A male voice started to cut through the static, "Sept, quarante-deux, onze."

Matt quickly scrambled over and slapped the power button, turning the radio off. He stood there for a moment just staring at the device. It took him a few seconds to realize it, but he was shaking. He quickly forced himself to calm down by taking a few deep breaths. Slowly, he sat down in his office chair as he tried to make sense of what just happened. After several minutes of contemplation, he determined that the power button must be sensitive. Every time he moved enough to cause some vibration across the table, he ran the risk of the device turning on.

Matt let out a small sigh of relief as the feeling of anxiety faded away with his explanation. He wasn't dealing with a sentient radio that was turning itself on. There was nothing he had to worry about besides a sensitive button on an antique piece of equipment. Once he had finally gotten up from his desk and started to make a sandwich, he realized that he should get some headphones. Court would not be very happy with him if the radio randomly came on during the night. He snarfed down his sandwich and quickly got dressed. He hustled out the front door, slamming it behind him.

The apartment was silent for a moment before the noise of static sounded. It filled the empty room space for ten minutes until Court opened the door. He stepped inside to discover the noise of crackling static and was immediately annoyed by it. He scanned the area for Matt but didn't see him. He moved over toward the bathroom, assuming that his roommate was there. Once he saw that there was no light coming from underneath the door, he headed for Matt's room.

"Matt!" he yelled in annoyance as he threw open the door, "Turn off your damn radio!"

He was surprised to see that the room was also empty. He stood in the doorway for a few moments then headed back out into the living room. Court walked to the desk and reached to turn off the device. As his finger was about to press the power button, the voice of a woman broke through the static and started calling out numbers. He hesitated for a moment then turned it off. As he was stepping back from the desk, the front door opened and Matt walked in.

The sudden appearance of his roommate startled Court for a moment, but he quickly recovered. "Your radio was turned on," he grumbled.

"Sorry about that," Matt hustled over. "I went to the store to get these bad boys," he said as he pulled a new set of headphones out of a plastic bag. Matt quickly ripped them out of their packaging and plugged them into the input on the radio. "There," he smiled, "Now if it randomly turns on in the middle of the night, we won't hear it."

"Wait, what?" Court asked in surprise, "It turns on randomly?"

"Yeah," Matt nodded, "The power button is really sensitive. It shouldn't be a problem with the headphones though."

"Right," Court said slowly. He stood there for a few moments then mentioned, "It was on one of those number stations."

"Really?" Matt turned to Court. With a clear tone of intrigue, he asked, "Did you hear anything?"

"Yeah," Court nodded, "It was just some lady reading off numbers though. It's not like anything cool happened."

"Oh, man! How the hell did I miss out on that?" Matt smiled, "I spent all night trying to hear something and you just happen to walk in on it the second I leave. If I were a betting man I'd say you were curious and decided to check it out for yourself." He slapped Court on the shoulder then turned and started to head toward his room. "Maybe there's still a chance I can get you invested in them."

"Keep dreaming," Court sarcastically replied. A slight ringing noise suddenly sounded in his left ear as Matt walked away. He dug his pinky finger into his ear canal to try to get the sound to stop. After a few seconds, the noise ceased on its own. Court rubbed his ear as he went into his room. "That was weird," he muttered to himself.

Matt let out a deep sigh as he stared blankly at his computer screen. After five hours of work, he had only managed to type out two pages. His report was all but dead in the water for the evening. He turned his head toward the radio and contemplated trying to find a number station again. After a minute or so of debating with himself, he put on his headphones and turned on the device.

He quickly had to turn down the volume as an immediate screech of static assailed his ears. Once he had gotten the noise issue under control, Matt started searching through the different frequencies. He was doubtful that he would be able to pick up anything as he hadn't been successful in doing so for a few days. After several minutes of messing with his tuning dial, he decided to call it quits. Just as he was reaching for the power button, a male voice cut through the static.

"Seven, forty-two, eleven," the voice calmly recited.

Matt quickly opened a new document on his computer and started to type down the numbers. He felt like he was making some real progress in getting things recorded around the time he typed the tenth number out. Before he could put more down, a light ringing sounded in his ears. He tried to ignore it while listening to the voice, but it quickly grew much louder. In a matter of seconds, he couldn't take the pain brought by the overpowering sound and threw off his headphones in desperation. He immediately squeezed his hands against his ears in an attempt to drown out the high-pitched noise.

The pain in Matt's ears started to migrate its way toward his brain, adding more intensity to the unpleasant sensation. He couldn't help but audibly gasp in agony as he cradled his head between his hands. The noise continued to grow higher in pitch with seemingly no end to it until suddenly, it came to an abrupt halt. Met by sudden silence, he sat still in complete disbelief that the ringing had ceased killing his ears. He slowly brought his hands down and breathed a sigh of relief.

"Oh, thank god that's over," he whispered to himself.

Matt lightly pushed away from his desk and prepared to stand up, but before he did, he caught sight of something out of the corner of his eye. He slowly rotated his head to the left as bubbling anxiety filled his stomach. The kitchen light gave just enough illumination for him to barely make out something in the entryway of the hall leading to Court's bedroom. As he spent several tense moments solely focused on it, his eyes started to pick up on the shadowy outline of a person just standing there. He felt the anxiety in his stomach twist itself into full-blown fear as his gaze remained fixed on the mysterious figure.

"W-who are you?" he weakly called out.

The unknown presence responded to Matt by taking just enough steps into the light to show itself to him. He gasped as he stared at the see-through being that was punctuated by a black outline surrounding it. It took another step toward him, and he realized that the anomaly was more akin to opaque than see-through in its unnatural appearance. The figure had a light gray color that filled in the void between the dark borders of its body. In the midst of his terror, he noticed that the outline of the thing seemed to be constantly moving as if the figure wasn't entirely there. The presence took another step forward and Matt closed his eyes while tensing up. He waited for the thing to attack him while he sat frozen in fear, but nothing happened. Cautiously, he opened his eyes to look at the spot where the figure had been and saw that it had vanished. He let out a sigh of relief an instant prior to the unnatural thing suddenly reappearing right in front of him.

"What are you!" he screamed as it grabbed his arms. "What do you want!"

A strange, screeching voice responded, "Numbers."

"W-what numbers," Matt whimpered, "Like the numbers from my birthdate? The pin to my debit card? What do you mean?"

"Numbers," the thing repeated.

"I-I don't know what that means!"

"Numbers!" it screamed at him as it pointed at his radio.

"The number stations?" Matt weakly asked.

The figure let go of him and slowly backed away. Matt watched as the thing just vanished into thin air, leaving him by himself. He violently trembled from the mix of terror and adrenaline flowing through his body. With trepidation, he looked back to see that his radio was still on and quickly switched it off. He wrapped his arms around himself in a feeble attempt at comfort. His eyes were constantly darting about the room, searching the area for any signs of where the figure could have gone. After a few minutes of shaking in his chair, he finally started to calm down. Suddenly, the front door to the apartment was thrown open and he jumped in fright. Court stumbled in and looked over to see his roommate staring at him. Matt slowly pulled himself out of his office chair as an inebriated Court closed the door.

"You doing okay?" Court asked with a hiccup.

Matt nodded as he walked past Court and checked to make sure the door was locked. He turned back to his friend while contemplating if he should tell him what he had just seen. "I-I heard the numbers," he stuttered.

"G-good for you man," Court lazily slapped his roommate on the shoulder.

"No, it's not," Matt said throwing Court's hand off him. He scrambled back to his desk and sat down. "I heard the numbers and then...then some...thing started hurting my ears."

"Psshhh, you just had your radio up too loud. I told you not to do that," Court said in a light scolding tone.

"It wasn't too loud!" Matt shouted. He turned to Court, "It was this weird ringing noise, and it kept getting higher and higher." He groaned in frustration, "And then I saw this thing."

"What kind of thing?" Court asked as he shuffled toward Matt.

"I-It was some kind of man...but not. He was like a shadow. At least...it seemed like he was."

"Oh! A spooky shadow man," Court laughed. He slapped Matt on the shoulder again, "H-have fun with the shadow man. I'm going to bed."

Matt anxiously watched Court lazily shuffle through the area the shadowy figure had come from. He held his breath for a few seconds as he waited to see if his roommate would be attacked. After several tense moments, he heard Court flopping down onto his bed and let out a sigh of relief. He shook his head as he turned around to see his computer still on. With a glance, he noticed the document he had written the numbers down on was clearly missing a few as there were only six on the page, and he could have sworn he had put more on there.

He racked his brain to try to remember what the missing numbers could have been, but he came up with nothing. Matt switched off the computer and rose to his feet. He went straight to his room and climbed into bed while still thinking about the thing that had attacked him. Eventually, once he had replayed the strange encounter in his mind well over a dozen times, he closed his eyes and tried to drift off while trying to picture something more pleasant. After several moments, a familiar voice echoed through his brain. It was reciting the numbers he had heard earlier. Constantly cycling through the numbers he remembered, it was eventually what put him to sleep.

Part 2

A Few Steps Down

Madison smiled as she reached across the table and gently placed her hand on Matt's. "Thanks for doing this, babe," she quietly said in a content tone.

"You're welcome," Matt nodded. "Completing midterms always requires a celebration."

"Preferably one with alcohol," Madison lifted her glass of wine and sipped. She leaned forward and whispered, "How can you afford this place? Everything on the menu is at least fifteen bucks."

Matt chuckled, "I've been doing a lot of tutoring since the semester started. Don't worry, I get paid enough for the rent and have a little extra left over for something like this."

Madison shook her head, "Matt, you don't have to spend all your money like this."

"I know," he smiled, "I want to do this." Matt gestured to the plate of shrimp carbonara sitting in front of Madison, "Now let's dig in!"

Madison stabbed her fork into the pasta and twisted the noodles around it. She brought it to her mouth and savored the flavor as she chewed on her food. After a few more bites she nodded her head in approval, "This is fantastic!"

"I'm glad you like it," Matt replied as he eagerly took a bite of his spaghetti.

Suddenly, as if to try to ruin the meal, a noise started to worm its way into Matt's left ear as he took another bite. He tried to ignore the noise and focus on his food, but the sound gradually started to get louder. The smile began to fade from his face as he began to hear the ringing in his right ear as well. He looked up to see Madison saying something to him, he assumed about the food, and he just nodded along with it. His level of discomfort began to grow in tandem with the ringing and he couldn't hide it on his face anymore as the pain started to truly manifest itself.

"Are you okay?" Madison quietly asked.

Matt grimaced as he put his hands over his ears, pressing the appendages firmly against the sides of his head. He took a deep breath and closed his eyes. His desperate attempts did absolutely nothing to stop the ringing from increasing in volume. He felt the pain grow sharper and harsher as it continued, sending rippling waves of agony through his ear canals. The sensation of someone touching his arm caused him to open his eyes and look to see Madison reaching across the table to check on him. She wore a look of concern as she stared at him. Then just like that, the ringing was suddenly gone, along with the pain that had come with it, as though it had been driven away by Madison's gentle touch. He blinked a few times then slowly brought his hands away from his ears.

"Are you okay?"

Matt nodded, "Um...yeah, I-I just have a bit of a headache is all. It's nothing to worry about."

"Matt, if you don't feel up for dining out, we can just take the food back to your place," Madison offered.

He shook his head, "No, it's fine." Matt sighed, "It was just a quick headache. It's gone now, I swear."

Madison sat back in her chair and stared at him for a moment before sighing. "Okay," she nodded. "It won't ruin my evening if we have to leave." She looked Matt in the eye, "You don't have to grind through the pain on my account."

He put on a fake smile, "Thank you, but I really am fine. It was just a small headache. I've been having them off and on for a little bit."

"Really?" Madison skeptically questioned, "You haven't ever had that problem before. When did these start happening?"

"Just a few days ago. They come and go, and they never last long. There's not much else to say about it really," he finished his response with a nonchalant shrug to sell that it was nothing to worry about. He made sure to leave out the parts about the ringing sound that always came before the headaches, and of course, how the pain all started right after the night he fell asleep while listening to a number station.

"Are you going to see someone about it?" Madison prodded.

"What, like a doctor?" Matt chuckled. "There's no reason to see a doctor. I bet it's all from stress."

"You think writing your paper is causing you to get headaches?" she asked with a hint of skepticism.

"Stress can do a lot of harm to the body," Matt shrugged. "It makes logical sense that I would be getting headaches from it." He quickly stuffed his mouth with a bite of food so they would stop talking about it.

Madison crossed her arms and sighed as she looked at her significant other. After a few moments, she unfolded her arms and picked up her fork. “You would tell me if there was something wrong, wouldn’t you?”

He swallowed the bit of food in his mouth and nodded, “Of course I would.”

Madison gave a small smile to his reply as she twirled some more noodles around her fork. Matt felt a sense of relief in having assuaged her concerns and looked down at his food. Just as he was about to go for another bite, a feeling of unease suddenly overcame him and he slowly sat down his fork. A notion that someone was watching him crept through his mind, and he desperately needed to make sure that wasn’t the case. He knew that frantically scanning the restaurant would put Madison on high alert, so he would have to be more discreet. Trying to be as inconspicuous as possible, he pretended to stretch his back so he could quickly peek over his shoulder. As he scanned the tables behind him, he didn’t see anything out of the ordinary.

Matt realized he must have just been feeling paranoid over nothing and turned back to Madison. He picked up his fork and smiled at her, then took another bite of his food and slowly chewed it. The familiar sensation of someone staring at him popped back up only seconds later, and in turn, brought his gaze away from his date toward the open space a dozen feet in front of him. That's when he saw the shadowy figure from his apartment, just standing there. The constant shifting of its dark outline didn't seem as severe as before, and it looked to be slightly opaquer than he remembered. The otherworldly being took a step forward and he let out an audible gasp of fear.

"What's up?" Madison asked upon seeing his face. She looked behind her and didn't spot anything except for a waiter making his way down the tables. When she turned back to her boyfriend, she found him still staring at the same spot as before. "Matt, are you sure you're okay?"

The figure took a few sudden steps toward their table, and he jumped a little bit. He felt the intensity of the gaze from the unnatural being, and his fear grew. Matt looked at the area the shadow was standing in front of and saw that none of the people sitting there seemed phased by it. He couldn't help but slam his palms onto the table in a terrified reaction as the shape took another step toward him.

"C-can you see it?" he desperately whispered to her.

She looked over her shoulder but still didn't identify anything out of the ordinary. "See what, Matt?" Madison turned back to him. "What am I supposed to be seeing?"

"The shadow," he whimpered, "There's a shadow that's coming right at us."

Upon his mentioning its presence, the figure sprinted the rest of the way to the table. Matt screamed out in fear at the sudden advancement from the ethereal thing as he brought his arms in front of his face. He leaned back too far in his chair and found himself tumbling backward onto the ground. Even though he was flooded with pain from the fall, he anxiously waited for the figure to grab ahold of him, but nothing happened. He lay on the ground, heavily breathing with his eyes closed for several more seconds. Slowly, he opened them and looked to see that the shadow had vanished. He quickly realized that most of the patrons of the restaurant were staring at him.

"Jesus, Matt! Are you okay?" Madison said as she rushed over to help him to his feet.

He shakily took her hand and stood up as he scanned the judging faces around him. Matt slowly nodded, "I'm...I'm fine." He let out a few trembling breaths before quietly saying, "I-I thought I saw something."

"Like what?" Madison responded with concern.

Matt shook his head, "N-Nothing. It was nothing."

Madison picked his chair off the floor and placed it back where it had been. She walked back to her seat and sat down. Matt stood there for a few moments with a mix of fear and shame washing over him. He finally went back to his seat and lowered his head.

"I'm so sorry," he quietly apologized.

Madison let out a deep sigh as she responded, "It's fine Matt. I'm more concerned about you than anything else right now."

"It was supposed to be a happy evening and I ruined it," Matt solemnly said. He slowly took his wallet out and pulled several twenties from it, setting them down on the table. "I'm sorry for destroying the night for you." He stood up to leave, "There's more than enough for dinner, and you could get some dessert if you want."

"What are you doing?" Madison snapped in frustration, "Why won't you tell me what's going on? You're freaking me out, Matt."

"I know," he nodded, "that's why I'm heading home. I don't want to scare you anymore."

He turned and fast-walked out of the restaurant, leaving Madison by herself. She sat at the table in shock for several moments as she stared down at her food. Finally, she stood up and ran out of the restaurant into the parking lot where she desperately scanned the filled spots for Matt's car, but wasn't able to find it. She eventually walked inside the restaurant and went back to her table.

"Is everything all right, madame?" the waiter asked.

"No, no it's not." She muttered as she looked at him, "But none of that is your fault. Can I get a to-go box?"

The waiter nodded, "Of course," and walked off.

She shook her head as she raised her glass and downed the rest of her wine.

Matt furiously typed the numbers being read out over the airwaves. There was nothing else on his mind than simply recording what the female voice said. His brain was completely void of any other thought as all focus was put on simply moving his fingers across the keys. The ringing noise had begun later than usual, but regardless, it had started to build over the past few minutes. He didn't know when the sound would overpower him, but he tried to muscle through it. A sudden tap on his shoulder caused him to jump in surprise, as well as pull his attention away from the numbers. He whipped his head around to see Court just standing there.

"What do you want?" he snapped as he pulled his headphones off.

"Jeez, I'm just checking in on you," Court responded while taking a step back. "You haven't said anything since you came back early from your date with Madison last night. I'm...I'm just kind of worried about you."

A twinge of guilt shot through Matt and he turned his chair to face his roommate. "Uh...I'm sorry about that. I was trying to type something out when you interrupted me."

"So, what happened last night?" Court asked while folding his arms.

"We went out for dinner. It was a nice meal and...that was that," Matt replied with a half-truth.

"Why didn't she come back here?" Court wondered. "I mean if the dinner was so nice, I would assume Madison would want to continue the date."

"Well, you assumed wrong," Matt growled. "She isn't that kind of lady."

"I didn't mean to offend," Court quickly took another step back. He scratched his chin as he continued, "I just wanted to know if there was anything else that may have been the reason the night ended so early."

"There wasn't," Matt snapped once again.

"So, nothing weird happened, huh?" Court took in a deep breath before slyly throwing out, "Nothing like you falling out of your chair because you saw something?"

Matt felt a wave of embarrassment hit him and he quietly asked, "Who told you?"

"Madison called me this morning 'cause she's worried about you," Court squatted down so he was at eye level with Matt. "She said you left in a hurry last night, and that you haven't been returning her calls. Why are you doing that, man?"

"I'm too embarrassed to answer them," Matt admitted. He shook his head, "I made a fool of myself in front of her and a restaurant full of people. I just...I just need a moment before I talk to her again."

"I guess I understand," Court said quietly as he stood up. He pointed at Matt. "You better not keep her waiting too long. If you do, you're gonna screw up things between you two. And you definitely don't want to do that."

"You're right," Matt reluctantly admitted, "I should just swallow my pride and call."

"Damn straight!" Court exclaimed while turning to leave the room. He looked back over his shoulder and asked, "So...what did you see last night?"

Matt sighed, "Court, do we have to talk..."

"I know you're embarrassed by it, but I'm not gonna laugh at you, bud. I'm just curious."

"Okay," Matt nodded. He hesitated for a moment but eventually relented, "I saw some sort of figure. It was like a shadow, but...not really. Plus, it seemed like it was sentient.

Like it had a mind of its own. I mean...it had to be...it came straight at me. I don't know, it's hard to explain."

"Well, have you seen this thing before?" Court asked as he turned back toward his roommate.

"I saw it here once but other than that, no. I mean, I told you about it, but I guess you were probably too drunk to remember." He forced a chuckle to make himself feel better. "I guess it's just been a weird week for me."

"I guess so," Court said in agreement.

"First, I get this ringing noise in my ears, and then I start having headaches. Now I'm seeing a shadow man who's trying to get me," Matt laughed. "I'm having a hell of a time."

"Did you say ringing?" Court asked with piqued interest.

"Yeah, I've had this weird ringing noise going on in my ears."

"Could you describe it?"

"It's a high-pitched sort of sound, that gets gradually louder," Matt shrugged. "That's it. I don't know how else to describe it."

Court nodded as he stared off for a moment. A bit of anxiety started to bubble in the pit of his stomach. He tried to sound as calm and collected as possible as he said, "That's interesting."

"Is it?" Matt said in confusion. "Why are you so interested?"

"I uh," Court coughed as he thought of something to say, "I recently read an article where they talked about some people who suffered from a mysterious ringing noise in their ears."

"What happened to them?"

"Oh um...they eventually got treated for it and it went away."

"Oh, well that's kind of anticlimactic."

"Yeah, I guess it is," Court agreed. "I was just curious to see if it had been the same thing, you know, that way you could get it treated."

Matt nodded, "Well I appreciate it."

"Yeah, no problem," Court replied. He did a fake stretch while giving a weak attempt at a yawn. "Welp, I'm pretty tired so I'm going to hit the hay."

"Okay," Matt nodded. "Sounds good."

Court hurried back into his room and shut the door. The feeling of dread was almost overwhelming as he paced across the floor. He was terrified at the idea that what was happening to Matt could happen to him. His roommate had been acting weird as of late, and after what Madison told him, he knew something was wrong. He didn't tell anyone, but he had experienced a ringing noise, oh so briefly, a few days ago. What if that was the early stages of the same thing affecting Matt? He didn't want to be seeing shadow people in his bedroom at night.

Court flopped onto his bed and stared up at the ceiling. "What the hell is happening?" he muttered to himself. He took in a few deep breaths to try to calm himself down as he repeated, "What the hell is happening?"

Professor Burrows continued to drone on as Matt fought to stay awake. He hadn't been able to get a good night's sleep for the past several days. The ringing in his ears had started to keep him awake for several hours each night. Not to mention, he couldn't help but think about the numbers during his every waking moment. The only reason he wasn't thinking about the stations right now was that he was fighting just to stay awake.

He started to close his eyes as he teetered toward losing consciousness. An elbow in his side snapped his head upward and he woke up a bit. He turned to his left to see Court giving him a look of concern, which he responded to by mouthing the word *sorry*. Matt shook his head a few times to clear some of the sleepiness away before turning his attention to Professor Burrows. Thanks to his sudden inclination for naps the past few days, he had significantly fallen behind in the class, and his hopes of catching up were diminishing with each lecture.

Picking up his pen, he started to mindlessly take down notes on the topic that was up on the board. He had no idea what any of it meant, but he assumed it was important. Matt steadied his notebook as he finished scribbling the last bit of a sentence. He brought his head up to see what else was on the board when he noticed something strange move behind Burrows. Immediately, he felt a twinge of fear as the hairs stuck up on the back of his neck. He watched, in sheer horror, as the shadow figure that had been after him slowly moved around the professor and into his field of view. Matt let out a stifled gasp of terror as the shape stared directly at him.

"What's wrong?" Court whispered.

"N-nothing," Matt stuttered.

"You just sounded like you've seen a ghost," Court hissed. "What's wrong?"

Matt frantically closed his journal and shoved it into his backpack. "I...uh...just really have to use the bathroom," he shakily responded as he stood up.

Matt clumsily made his way past the classmates in the row he was on, tripping over several of them. He managed to exit out onto the stairs, where he looked toward Professor Burrows to see that the shadow had progressed to the bottom of the steps. The ethereal being slowly started to make its way toward him, filling him with fear and causing his body to lock up for a moment. A quick shot of adrenaline snapped him out of it, and he immediately bounded up the steps. He brazenly threw open the doors of the lecture hall and raced into the atrium.

After taking a few seconds to calm his nerves down, he started to head for the front doors inconspicuously so as not to have any passersby questioning his sanity. He stopped dead in his tracks when he noticed the shadowy figure standing just before the front doors. *How did it beat me here*, he thought to himself. He had sworn that he had managed to move fast enough to ditch the ethereal being that was after him in the lecture hall. Matt took a closer look at the unnatural thing a few dozen feet in front of him, and just barely noticed the minute differences of the entity. It was slightly smaller than the shadow that normally came after him, and this one had a wider outline. He took a timid step back in horror upon realizing that there was more than one of the ethereal creatures that existed.

Matt turned and started to sprint for an exit down the left hallway when he saw another dark figure coming from that way. His gaze shot between the two shadows in absolute disbelief at what was happening. A sensation of something coming up from behind had him looking over his shoulder to see the third shadow phase through the lecture hall doors. He stumbled off to the right as the three figures started to move in.

"Numbers...numbers," the closest figure to him said in a crackling, low voice.

"S-stay a-away from me!" Matt whimpered. He frantically backed up a few more feet before screaming, "What do you want!"

"Numbers," the shadows joined together in unison. "Numbers."

He turned and sprinted for the exit that was down the hall. His shoes squeaked against the tile as he moved. While he was running, a random door swung open and a professor stepped out to see what the commotion was. Matt saw her but couldn't stop in time. He collided with the unprepared educator and sent her to the ground, while he tumbled over her smaller frame. Matt frantically pushed himself up off the floor and glanced back at where he had come from to see the shadows gaining ground.

"What the hell are you doing?" the professor demanded to know.

"They're after me!" Matt yelled as he scrambled to his feet and took off.

He bolted the last fifty feet to the metal doors of the exit and threw them open. Matt tripped down the stairs and busted his right knee pretty badly on the concrete. He let out a cry of pain as he cradled his injury while a wave of agony shot up his leg. While howling in pain, he glanced up from his wound just in time to see the first of the shadows phase through the metal doors. A second shot of adrenaline surged through him and helped to pull his mind off his agony. He frantically crawled back across the concrete as the otherworldly thing descended the steps.

It took some desperate clawing, but he finally managed to scramble far enough away that he had time to pick himself up from the slow advancing shadow. With a great deal of effort, he stumbled onto his feet and pushed forward just before the ethereal being could reach him. He took off in a dead sprint through the college campus, his lungs burning from the early winter air that he was forced to rapidly breathe in. He hadn't run in a very long time, so after a minute or two, his legs joined his lungs in feeling like they were on fire. Matt looked ahead to the hill he would have to run up to reach the parking lot where his car was. A feeling of doubt washed over him as he started up the enormous obstacle.

He struggled to gain ground on the incline, and in turn, his speed greatly suffered for it. His body couldn't bear the climb and he stopped for a minute or so. Matt looked over his shoulder to see the three, unnatural figures moving across the campus at a brisk pace. They were a good two hundred feet from him and closing in fast. He quickly built his resolve up and pushed himself up the hill. His calves ached as he continued his drive up the steep incline. With a final short burst of all his energy, he stumbled up to the top of the hill. He took in gasps of desperate air as he wasted no time and hustled to his car.

Matt hopped inside his vehicle and threw off his backpack. He frantically dug around in his pockets as he searched for his keys. His fingers bumped into the familiar, metal object and he pulled them out. He looked toward the hill and didn't see any of the figures coming to the top of it yet. With a twinge of hope, he shoved his keys into the ignition and violently turned them. The engine sputtered for a few seconds but didn't turn on. He slammed his fists against the steering wheel in a brief moment of frustration then tried it again. After a few seconds, the engine groaned before finally roaring to life.

He laughed in relief as he quickly put the car in reverse. While he was backing up, the shadows finally reached the top of the hill. Matt saw them quickly approaching him and put the car in drive. He spun out of the parking lot and headed off the campus, leaving the inhuman things behind. As he drove, he continued to stare at them in his rearview mirror, just to make sure he was truly getting away. He let out a deep sigh as he realized that he couldn't go back to his apartment just yet. The shadows would most certainly follow him there if he did.

Court heard a knock at the front door and slowly shuffled out of his room. There was another set of knocks that quickly grew into banging by the time he had made it to the entryway. He sighed heavily before opening the door to find Madison with a look of worry on her face.

"Madison?" Court said in surprise. "What are you doing here?"

"I was hoping Matt was around," she replied.

"Well, did you call him and ask?"

"No," Madison shook her head, "he hasn't returned any of my calls for the past few days now."

Court looked at his feet for a second while he thought about what he should do. He opened the door a little further. "Well, I don't think he's here, but you're more than welcome to see."

"Thank you." Madison gave a small smile as she pushed past him. She made her way through the living room and to the small hallway that led to Matt's bedroom. The door was shut, so she lightly knocked on it. "Matt?" she called out. "Matt, are you there?"

After receiving no response, Madison sighed in frustration and shuffled out into the living room. Court gave her a small nod while wearing a straight face that showed no emotion. She walked over and slowly sat down on the lone couch. Court stood there for a moment and then reluctantly took a seat at the opposite end. An awkward silence hung in the air as the two stared off in completely different directions from each other with no idea what to say. There was a strange tension between them, as they had never been in the same room together without Matt being present.

"I just don't get it," Madison finally broke the silence. "I've been with Matt for almost two years now, and he's never acted like this," she groaned in frustration. "He's always answered my calls, even if he was busy. I never thought he would do something like walk out on me during dinner and then ghost me." She looked at Court, "Why the hell is he acting this way? Did I do something wrong?"

Court sighed as he looked down at his feet. "No," he quietly replied, "you didn't do anything wrong." He brought his gaze up to meet Madison's. "Matt is doing all this to himself."

"All of what?" Madison asked in frustration. "What possible plan could he have that calls for him to act like a dick to me?"

Court shrugged. "I don't know what his endgame is to be honest. I just know that he's been acting weird lately."

"You got that right," Madison muttered under her breath. She thought for a moment, then asked, "Have you been able to reach him?"

Court shook his head, "No, I haven't seen him since this morning. I've called him a few times, but he hasn't picked up."

"Where was he when you saw him last?"

"In class," Court flatly answered after a moment of hesitation.

Madison could tell there was more to it and pressed, "Did something happen in said class?"

Court scrunched his face as he responded, "I really shouldn't be saying anything."

"Tell me Court!" Madison pressed. "I need to know."

"Fine, okay," Court gave in. "He was falling asleep in class today. I kept having to elbow him to keep him awake. He suddenly got wide-eyed, like he had seen something. Then he told me he had to go to the bathroom and sprinted out of the lecture hall."

"I take it he didn't come back to class," Madison remarked.

"He...did not," Court sighed. "Plus, everyone heard him screaming in the hallway like two minutes after he left."

"He was screaming in the hallway?" Madison repeated in alarm. "Why are you being so nonchalant about it? Don't you think something could have happened to him?" Court remained silent and she lightly slapped his shoulder. "Don't you care about him?"

"Of course I do!" he snapped. He immediately regretted raising his voice. Court lowered his volume and said, "He's my roommate and my friend. I care about him." He paused before lightly saying, "I just...also know that he hasn't been all there mentally...as of late."

"What the hell are you talking about?"

"He told me what he saw at the restaurant that spooked him so much," Court quietly replied.

"What?" Madison said leaning toward Court.

"I'll tell you, but you can't say it was me that did, agreed?"

Madison nodded, "Yeah, that's fair."

Court shook his head as he reluctantly said, "He saw...a shadow and...he said that it was after him."

"A shadow?" a confused Madison mumbled.

"Yeah," Court nodded. "From what Matt said to me, he made it seem like there was a shadow that was trying to get him." He paused then added, "And it wasn't the first time he saw it either."

"He saw it before? When?"

"I can't say when," he replied, "but I know he saw it while sitting at his desk." He pointed to Matt's setup before continuing, "He was so embarrassed about what happened that he couldn't stand to talk to you about it. That's why he wasn't returning your calls...at first anyways." Court stroked his chin, "I honestly don't know why he's doing it now though."

"I don't understand," Madison stammered in disbelief. "Why is this happening to him? Why is he seeing these...shadows?"

"I don't know," Court shrugged, "he was completely fine until he got that radio." He thought about it for a moment before muttering, "That's when he started searching for number stations."

Madison caught some of what Court had mumbled and asked, "Did you say number stations?"

"Have you heard of them?" Court inquired, a bit surprised.

"Just what Matt has told me about them, which...I guess is a good amount," Madison said as she shook her head. "I know he wanted to get that radio so he could finally hear one of them. It was supposed to just be a curiosity thing. A dumb hobby." Madison looked at Court, "Do you think the number stations could be doing this to him?"

"I-I can't be sure," Court stammered. "Correlation doesn't equal causation but..." he paused for a second, "he didn't start acting weird until after he listened to one of the transmissions." He shook his head. "It doesn't make sense that just hearing someone say a bunch of numbers would do that to him. But I don't like to think about the alternative to that."

"You mean that he could be going crazy all on his own," Madison replied in a grave tone.

Court nodded, "Yeah, that wouldn't be good."

Madison stood up off the couch and folded her arms. "I'm worried, Court. He's out there, somewhere, seeing shadow people, and we have no idea where he is." She looked out the living room window and meekly squeaked out, "What if something happens to him?"

"Don't say that," Court said putting a hand on her shoulder. "Worrying like that isn't going to do you any good." He gently turned Madison toward him, "He's gonna be okay. Even if he is going crazy, Matt is the smartest guy I know. He wouldn't do anything stupid."

Madison slowly nodded. "You're right," she sighed. "He's probably off somewhere clearing his head." She walked past Court and headed to the front door. "That's what he always does," she said to herself while sucking in a few deep breaths to calm down. When she finally got her emotions under control, she glanced over her shoulder at Court. She shot him a weak smile, "Thanks for talking with me."

He gave a small head nod in response. "No problem."

"Will you do something for me?"

"What is it?"

"Call me the second he comes back."

Court gave an awkward thumbs up. "I will."

"Thank you," Madison quietly said as she opened the door and walked out.

Court shook his head as he shut the door behind her. *What a mess,* he thought to himself.

Court awoke to the sound of the front door opening. He leapt out of his bed and sprinted into the living room, still in a groggy state. In a mix of surprise and anger, he watched as Matt shuffled into the kitchen while not bothering to close the door behind him. Matt shared a moment's glance with him then started opening up one of the cabinets and pulling down a jar of peanut butter. Court quickly moved over and shut the front door with a sigh of agitation. He looked toward the kitchen to see that his roommate had gotten himself a spoon and was using it to eat from the jar.

"Where the hell have you been?" Court growled.

"I've been hiding out," Matt calmly replied.

"Hiding out?" Court scoffed. "From what? The shadow people?"

"Yes," Matt nodded as he slathered his tongue across the peanut butter-covered spoon.

"You can't do this man!" Court suddenly shouted.

"Do what?"

"You can't start acting weird and then just disappear." Court lowered his voice, "You know Madison has been worried sick about you."

Matt stared at Court for a long moment then replied, "I thought she would." He swallowed hard as he set the spoon down on the counter. "I knew I couldn't tell her what's really going on. She wouldn't be able to understand...and it would make things worse."

Court grimaced before he reluctantly admitted, "I told her everything, man."

"What do you mean?"

"I mean...everything," Court paused, then slowly continued, "about the number stations, and you...seeing the shadow people."

"Why would you do that!" Matt screamed in anger. "You have no right to do that! I told you that in secrecy and you went behind my back and told Madison!"

"Yeah, I did," Court responded firmly. "I had to because you decided to just run out of class and disappear for the whole day. I didn't know what the hell had happened to you. And Madison certainly didn't know either. So yeah, I told her. But you've got no one to blame but yourself."

"Why would you do that!" Matt slammed his fists against the counter. "Now she thinks I'm crazy!"

"No, she doesn't," Court growled. "She just wants to make sure that you're okay. If anything, she thinks you're an asshole for not returning her calls."

Matt narrowed his eyes as he stared daggers at his roommate, "Seems like you had a pretty nice conversation with her while I was gone." He slowly moved around the counter. "Sounds like you know a lot about what Madison has been up to lately." Matt scanned the room before asking, "Did she come by here?"

"Yeah," Court replied, "looking for you, you moron. Of course, you weren't here, so I told her I would call the second you came home." He shook his head. "Which I haven't done yet, by the way, because you're being ridiculous."

"Me?" Matt screamed. "I'm being ridiculous?" he scoffed. "That's hilarious coming from the guy who's trying to screw my girlfriend!"

"What the hell are you talking about?" Court asked in disbelief.

"I'm not stupid!" Matt shouted in anger. "She's been calling you, and then she conveniently shows up today when I'm not here."

"You weren't here because you disappeared, you idiot! That's the only reason Madison showed up! She was looking for you!" Court screamed back in frustration.

"Just admit it! You're sleeping with her!"

Court shook his head as he tried to calm down before speaking again. In a calmer voice, he said, "I'm not sleeping with Madison. We're both worried about you. That's the sole reason we've been talking to each other."

"You've been talking, which means you've been flirting," Matt yelled, "and I know what flirting leads to!"

"Did you hear anything of what I just said?" Court snapped with his voice rising a bit, "We've been worried about you. That's all!"

"I've had enough of your lies, you filthy cheater!" Matt screamed as he charged toward his roommate.

Matt swung at Court but only hit air as his roommate managed to duck just in time. Court responded to the act of aggression by delivering an uppercut that lifted Matt off the ground by a few inches. Matt fell onto the floor, with his back hitting the ground hard. He coughed as some of the air was knocked out of him. The injured man grimaced as he rolled onto one side and placed a hand against the spot on his back that was hurting. He felt something warm run down his chin and realized that the blow had busted open his lip.

Court stood over Matt with his fists raised to let his roommate know he would deck him if he stood up. The two stared at each other in tense silence. Matt brought his free hand to his face and slowly wiped the blood off his chin. He gave a hateful glare at Court and cautiously started to stand up. His roommate took a step toward him with his fists still raised and Matt stopped getting up.

"I didn't want to do that," Court said.

"Yeah right," Matt spat, "you're just trying to make me think I'm going crazy."

"Matt," Court said through gritted teeth, "I'm only going to say this once, so listen." He took in a deep breath and then started his rant. "You've been acting like a manic for over a week now. You're skipping classes and staying up late. Even when you do show up, you fall asleep five minutes into a lecture. You've been isolating yourself from everyone who cares about you and you're acting like a prick!" He pointed at Matt, "I'm not trying to sleep with Madison. But if you don't stop acting like a dick you will lose her. And if you don't pull yourself together real quick, I'm going to have to beat you until you do."

Matt couldn't help but feel hurt by Court's words. He sat there in silence for a few moments as he processed what his friend had just yelled at him and contemplated if he wanted to take another hit. Matt finally responded by quietly saying, "You're right. I have been acting like a dick." He stared up at his roommate. "I'm just so scared, Court. I-I don't know what's happening to me. I don't know why I'm seeing these things." He fearfully whimpered, "Am I going insane?"

Court held out a hand to help Matt up. "It's okay, man," he said pulling his friend off the floor. "You're going through a lot right now, but you've got me and Madison for support. We're here for you. We'll get through this."

Matt nodded, "Thank you." He slowly wrapped his arms around Court in an awkward hug. "I'm so glad you're my friend," he whispered.

Court didn't know what to say to that, so he just let Matt continue to hug him. After a few awkward seconds, he gently pushed himself back a bit and Matt let go of him.

He smiled as he said, "I'm gonna go give Madison a call and let her know you're back." He patted his friend on the shoulder. "Go get some sleep man, you need it."

Matt nodded as he watched Court turn and walk off. He stood there in the living room replaying the past few minutes in his mind. A feeling of sadness bubbled up inside of him as he realized he had hurt Court and Madison by suddenly disappearing for several hours. He wished that they could understand why he did it, but he knew they wouldn't be able to. No matter how hard he tried, there would be no way to show them what he was going through. He looked over at his desk and stared at the radio until an idea popped into his head. If Court heard the numbers, he might be able to understand what Matt had been going through. Maybe Court could help if he was in the same boat as him.

Quietly, he shuffled over to his desk and unplugged his headphones from the radio. He powered on the device and turned up the volume button. Matt quickly switched it back off before the static could annoy Court. He pivoted and moved toward the bathroom to clean the blood off himself. As he splashed water on his face, he knew the radio would randomly turn on during the night. Even if his roommate was asleep, he would be able to hear the numbers. He smiled at his reflection. Court would finally understand.

Part 3

A Friend's Descent

Court looked up from his notes and scanned the lecture hall for any sign of Matt. He shook his head in disappointment when he couldn't see him anywhere. In a bit of misplaced hope, he had honestly thought that his friend would start going back to class after he yelled at him, but that obviously wasn't the case. Granted, it had only been a few days since his roommate had reappeared, but he was still acting strange. Matt had continued to stay in the apartment all day. He spent all his time at his desk, just staring at his computer screen and listening to the static on his radio.

Suddenly, Court realized he had been lost in thought thinking about his friend and had missed something important that his professor had said. He sighed as he hastily tried to catch up on his notes while the educator was on a quick tangent. Silently his mind turned from the lecture as he told himself that Matt had to want to get better before anything would happen. Though, if he was being honest, Court wanted nothing more than for his friend to just magically be better. For things to just go back to the way they were, so he could focus on his classes without having to worry about his roommate. Even though that was his hope, he wasn't going to hold Matt's hand and force him to stop searching for number stations. There was too much for him to worry about to drop everything and turn all his attention to his pal.

A sudden but small ringing noise in his left ear caused Court to pause in his notetaking for a moment. It was the same sound he had been worried about a week ago but had managed to push to the back of his mind. The strange thing was, it had gone away for a few days, yet now it was coming back, much more frequently than before. He tried his hardest to ignore the noise as he continued to scribble down some notes. A similar ringing went off in his right ear and its addition made taking notes a lot harder. Through sheer stubbornness, he continued to write down what was on the board, while the ringing increased in volume until he couldn't hear the scribbling of his pen on the notebook.

He shook his head for a second in the hopes that it would stop the insufferable noise, but it didn't. Court took a deep breath while he tried to keep writing. The sound escalated its volume in both of his afflicted appendages and quickly reached the point where he couldn't hear the professor at all. He brought his left hand up and covered his ear as he kept trying to take notes. Pain started to build in both ears while the ringing also began to increase in pitch, getting higher and higher in frequency. He sat his pen down and brought his right hand up to cover his other afflicted appendage. With a scowl across his face, he closed his eyes and sat there with both ears covered.

Court's attempts to stop the ringing were all in vain as it kept growing louder. He started to shake as the pain grew to an intolerable level. Unable to stop it, he let out a gasp of agony, and the student sitting next to him shot a side-eye glance his way. Finally, he couldn't take it anymore, there was too much pain. Quickly, he stood up and forced his way to the end of the row. He moved up the stairs, trying to climb them at a normal pace. As soon as he exited the lecture hall, he took off sprinting.

Running at full speed, he burst into the bathroom and ran over to the nearest sink. He dug his fingers into his ears as a desperate way to force the ringing out. After a few attempts, he knew that wasn't going to work and fell to his knees as the pain riddled his brain with an unescapable headache. Just as he was nearing the verge of tears, the unbearable assault abruptly stopped. He sat there on the bathroom floor, waiting to see if the sound would return, but it didn't. Court was so happy that the pain was gone he started to chuckle.

"It's gone," he whispered to himself as he got to his feet.

He looked at his reflection in the mirror and noticed the sweat dripping down his cheeks. Court turned on the sink and placed his head under the running water. The cool liquid brought relief to his face as it washed over him. After a few seconds, he brought his head out from beneath the faucet and placed his hands under the running water. He eagerly cupped the cool liquid in his hands and brought it up to splash his face with. It was something he had done plenty of times before, but for some reason, it was much more enjoyable at that particular moment.

He took several more handfuls to splash his visage with. At this point, water was dripping down his face and neck. The top of his shirt was drenched in liquid, but he kept splashing water on himself anyway. After a few more rounds, he finally turned off the sink. He stood there, looking down into the basin and watching the liquid drain. Court slowly brought his gaze up to the mirror and stared at himself. He studied his drenched features and chuckled a little bit. A small streak of red off to the back of his left cheek caught his eye. He slowly turned his head, and to his abject horror, discovered that blood was running out of his ear.

Gasping, he quickly cupped his hand over his ear and stumbled over to the nearest stall. He threw open the door and slammed the toilet seat down. Without hesitation, he plopped down onto the porcelain seat before ripping a chunk of toilet paper off and stuffing it into the bleeding orifice. He sat there in shock, taking in several deep breaths. Court held out his hands in front of him and watched as they trembled. He tried to stop the shaking but couldn't.

Court didn't realize it until he sat down, but it was as if all his energy had been drained out of him. His legs felt like blocks of concrete had been attached to them, making it a struggle just to move the worn-out appendages. He leaned against the back of the toilet and tried to focus on calming down. Whatever had just happened to him, there would be time to figure it out later. For now, all he needed to do was relax for a moment. After taking a few more deep breaths, he finally felt calm. He went to stand up but found his body wouldn't obey his commands. Court tried again but to no avail. His eyelids started to feel heavy and he couldn't stop them from closing. In a matter of seconds, he drifted off to sleep.

Court scanned the books on the shelf in front of him, trying to find the right one. He ran his hands across each bit of binding to help him in his search. After a few seconds, he stumbled across an attractive red covering and pulled the book out. Wasting no time, he went back to the table where he had left his stuff and placed the find on top of the others. He hustled his way back through the rows to the section he had just been in. A glance at his phone told him he only had thirty minutes before the library closed, to find the last of the books he would need to finish his research.

As he frantically scanned a new row, he carefully brought his hand up and touched his left ear. A slight tingling of pain let him know that it was still sore from earlier in the day. He sighed and tried to focus on the task at hand. The sooner he found what he was looking for, the sooner he could get home and end this crappy day. Not only had he experienced excruciating pain that made his ear bleed, but he had also managed to fall asleep in a public bathroom for three straight hours. By the time someone had woken him up, it was late in the afternoon and he had missed his last class of the day. That's why he was at the library so late. He had planned on going there in between his classes, but thanks to his impromptu nap, that didn't happen.

Court yanked his last find off the shelf as his annoyance steadily grew with each passing moment. This was only further compounded when the book slipped from his fingers. His impulses almost got the better of him as he went to kick the book across the floor, but he managed to stop himself at the last second. Taking in a deep breath to calm himself, he slowly bent down and picked up the important bit of text. He brushed off the cover before tucking it under his arm and started to head back through the rows of shelving. That was the last one he needed, so now he just had to grab his things and he was headed home.

As he walked through the business section lined with rarely used items, a feeling of sudden unease came over him. He sensed that someone was lurking somewhere nearby. Court scanned the area around him but didn't immediately see anyone there. After having another look around, he decided that there wasn't anyone there and kept moving. A second later, the hairs stood up on the back of his neck and he knew a pair of eyes were looking right at him. He whipped his head around, but yet again, he didn't spot anyone.

"Hello?" he asked in a constrained voice.

No response came, but he was skeptical that there wasn't someone close by. He shook his head and started moving with a little bit more haste in his step. *Calm down,* he told himself. The library was still open, so there were probably some bookworms searching around in the sections of dusty tomes. He tried to convince himself that someone was just perusing about and nothing else. Though Court couldn't seem to shake the sensation of being watched and he started to move a little faster. The more he tried to convince himself that nothing was wrong, there more it felt like something was. He still felt a pair of eyes constantly staring at him as he continued to pick up the pace. Finally, having enough of the game someone was playing with him, he stopped dead in his tracks and spun around. His eyes quickly scanned the area and noticed a bit of movement from the opposite side of a shelf that was two rows back from him.

"I know you're there!" he shouted. After a few seconds, he asked, "Why are you following me?" He immediately became frustrated when whoever it was didn't answer. "Come on out!" he shouted. "Tell me what you want!"

Court stood his ground and waited for the creeper to step out from behind their hiding spot. His confidence quickly faded as he noticed an opaque, grey arm surrounded by a black outline poke out into his view. The rest of the figure gradually emerged from its hiding spot and he let out an audible gasp in horror as he realized what he was looking at. He stood there, in stunned silence, just staring at a sentient shadow. It was in that moment, that he realized that Matt had been telling the truth. The figure took a step forward and he immediately tensed up.

"W-What do you want?" he stammered.

The ethereal being lifted its arm and pointed at Court. A crackling and low voice said, "Numbers."

"What?" Court responded in confusion as he took a step back.

"Numbers," the shadow said again as it took a few steps toward him.

"S-stay away from me!" Court shouted as he backed up. "D-don't come any closer!"

The presence didn't seem to listen and kept slowly advancing toward him. Court took a step back and tripped over a small stool, falling to the ground. He looked up to see the shadow still progressing forth at a constant pace. Suddenly, a jolt of adrenaline overtook his fear and he quickly scrambled to his feet. He took off at a full sprint down the aisle as the ethereal thing continued to move at the same, consistent pace. After only a few seconds he was breathing heavily, while his legs started to ache and he felt all his energy start to fade away.

He looked ahead to see the opening from the shelves that led to the desks in the front area and felt a spark that pushed him to keep moving forward. He sprinted the last few feet out into the open just as the librarian was coming to check on all the noise. The two collided with each other and the older woman was knocked to the ground. Court stood there for a moment before realizing what he had done. He quickly held out a hand to help her up.

"There's no running in the library," she hissed as Court helped her to her feet.

"Yes, I know. I'm sorry," Court quickly apologized. He frantically glanced behind him and saw that the shadow was still progressing forth. He pushed past the librarian and sprinted to his stuff.

"I just said there's no running!" the librarian yelled. "If you don't stop, I'm going to have to ban you!"

"Look," Court growled, "I don't have time to explain, but there's something back there. Something...dark, something bad, and it's coming for me."

"What?" the librarian asked in confusion.

"I can't explain," Court said as he shoved the rest of his things into his backpack and slung it over his shoulder. "I'm sorry for running," he said as he took off for the front doors.

Court sprinted out of the library and ran down the concrete steps. He took a second to catch his breath as he looked back at the building. Anxiously, he watched to see if the shadow was still following him. After a few minutes had gone by and nothing appeared, he finally let out a sigh of relief. He turned and started walking across campus as his mind raced. What was that thing? Why was it after him? He knew that Matt might be able to give him some answers.

Matt's fingers flew over the keys as the numbers seemed to flow from the radio and into his head. Over the past few days, he had noticed the ringing in his ears was starting to dissipate, and on top of that, he hadn't seen a single shadow. It was like he was starting to build a tolerance to the number stations. He could listen for almost an hour now as numbers were called out over the airwaves. His sole focus was on finally getting everything typed out onto a single document instead of small bits of it spread over dozens of different files. As he worked, his computer's fan roared while it tried to keep the device from overheating, but it was a tall order due to the fact that it had been kept on for well over a week.

A knock at the door broke his concentration for a moment, which caused him to miss a number. He reacted to this by slamming his fists on the desk as he let out a grunt of anger. Matt stood up and threw his headphones onto the desk. He stomped over to the door and stood in front of it for a few seconds. For a moment, he debated just ignoring whomever it was and going back to the number station, but he had already missed too much. He ground his teeth together as he slowly unlocked the door and opened it.

"Madison," he said with a layer of surprise to cover the light twinge of annoyance in his voice. "What are you doing here?"

"I came to check up on you," she said with a forced half-smile. Madison stared at Matt, waiting for him to let her in. Finally, she took the initiative. "May I come in?"

Matt looked over his shoulder at the radio that was still turned on. After debating what to do for a moment, he looked at his girlfriend and nodded. "Yeah, come on in."

Madison stepped over the threshold into the apartment as she looked at her supposed beau awkwardly holding the door out of the corner of her eye. She took several steps toward the living room while waiting to hear the door close. Once she was sure he had shut it, she turned around to face him. "So how are things going?" she quietly asked.

"Oh uh...good, I guess," Matt coughed. "What about with you?"

"Things are fine." Madison looked at her feet. "A few of my classes are getting harder than expected."

"You'll be okay," Matt smiled. "You're the smartest person I know."

"You know I miss you," she said, taking a step closer toward him.

"Oh yeah?" he meekly replied.

"Of course," Madison said reaching out a hand toward him. She watched as he took a half step back from her and a strong, emotional hurt hit her in the chest. "Did...did I do something wrong, Matt?" she asked in a wavering tone.

"What do you mean?"

"I mean, you're still not answering my calls. You haven't seen me in over a week and the second I try to touch you you're backing away. Did I do something to upset you?"

Matt furiously shook his head. "No, no you didn't do anything."

"Then what's wrong?" Madison asked in concern.

"It's the numbers," he blurted out. "I'm working on getting all the numbers."

"What numbers? Are you talking about the number stations?" Madison shook her head. "Court told me you found a radio."

"I did!" Matt said excitedly, "It was cheap, and it works great. There was some difficulty finding the damn things at first, but now I can find a number station after a few minutes." He smiled. "I really think I'm getting close. I was making quite a dent in it before you knocked."

"What are you talking about? A dent in what?"

"I'm talking about actually writing down all the numbers that they say." Matt moved over to his desk and pointed at his computer. "I've been making steady progress on it."

"How often do you do this?" Madison asked as she cautiously approached the computer.

"Whenever I have free time," Matt answered as he sat down in his chair. He picked up his headphones then turned around and held them out toward her. "It's still on. Do you want to listen?"

"No, I don't," Madison quickly replied. She took a deep breath before asking, "How are classes going Matt?"

There was an awkward quiet that fell over the room as he slowly turned away from Madison and toward his radio. He started to randomly fiddle with dials on his setup in an attempt to dodge the question.

"Are you going to class, Matt?" Madison grew frustrated and finally said in an accusing tone, "You're not, are you?"

"No, I'm not," he snapped at her. "I have more important things to worry about than class."

"Matt," she began, "there are more important things than this hobby."

He whirled around in the chair and shouted, "It's not just a hobby!" He slammed his right hand on the desk, "You don't understand and you never will! There's something in these numbers. There's a hidden meaning that needs to be uncovered."

Madison took a few steps back as she was taken off guard by the sudden anger in Matt's voice. "If there is a hidden meaning," she paused, "if there is something to be found in all these numbers...why do you want to find it so bad?"

"Because I'm the only one who has the ability!" Matt shouted. "The shadows have come to me because I'm getting closer to figuring it out. They want me to find the truth. They need me to." He looked at Madison with a fierce intensity in his eyes. "I can't stop now! I have to finish it."

"What happens when you write down all the numbers? Will you stop?"

"Who knows?" he smiled. "That's the whole point of it being a mystery."

"You're scaring me, Matt," Madison took another step back, "You're obsessed. You have to stop."

"Have you not been listening to a word I was saying!" he screamed. He took a few quick steps toward the back-tracking Madison. "I can't stop! Until all the numbers are written down, this will not end!"

"That's not true, you can stop right now." Madison took another step back and found her left heel smacking against the front door. She gasped as Matt came closer, and in a knee-jerk reaction, she placed her back flat against the door. "The numbers don't mean anything!" she yelled.

He leaned forward and slammed his left hand against the door, right next to Madison's face. "They mean everything!" he growled, "The universe. The meaning of life. How the earth will end. All of those could be what the numbers explain. I need answers." He leaned in closer. "You will not stop me!"

"No!" Madison screamed before kicking Matt in the shin. She saw he was off balance and forcefully pushed him away from her.

As he fell to the floor, she turned and threw the door open. Matt watched from the floor as Madison ran out of the apartment and disappeared from his view. He groaned as he picked himself up and hobbled over to shut the door.

"She doesn't understand," he mumbled. "None of them do." He made his way over to his desk and sat down, "But

I do." He cracked a smile. "As long as I do, that's all that matters."

The occasional flash of illumination from the streetlights was doing nothing to diffuse the anxiety that Court was feeling. His eyes constantly scanned the sides of the road, looking to see if there were any of those shadows waiting for him. He fought with all his might to focus on something else, but his mind would always come back to the thing he saw in the library. Fear constantly flowed through his body, making his limbs uncontrollably shake. To make matters worse, a bubbling sense of dread in his gut had his stomach tossing about, making him queasy as he drove along.

Court felt the constant perspiration his hands were emitting over the steering wheel, making the smooth surface slick. He wiped his left hand on his pants, and then his right. His left leg shook continuously as he put most of his efforts into just trying to keep his right one still. All the while, his eyes were constantly moving in search of anything out of the ordinary. During a glance to his left, he noticed a dark figure start to emerge into the light under a streetlamp. He audibly gasped in fear as he thought he had spotted another of the ethereal beings.

As his car raced by the figure, it became apparent that it was just a man in a dark hoodie. Court let out a sigh of relief before he turned his attention back toward the road. He was greeted by a pair of headlights, which were pointed right at him, making it nearly impossible to see. In a split second, he realized the lights were heading straight toward him. Quickly, he turned his steering wheel to the right and narrowly avoided a head-on collision as he swerved back into his lane. Adrenaline raced through his body from the sheer terror of narrowly avoiding death, which caused his hands to shake even more uncontrollably than before.

Court felt his heart beating so hard against his chest that it was starting to hurt. He thought there was a good possibility he was having a heart attack. With all the internal chaos he was experiencing, he knew he couldn't keep driving in his current condition and immediately turned down the first street he saw that led into a residential area. He continued driving for a few hundred feet then slammed on the brakes and turned off the vehicle. Immediately after the engine stopped running, he threw open the car door and frantically took off his seatbelt. He stumbled out of the vehicle and desperately gasped in the cool, night air.

The adrenaline was still surging through him, so his legs were trembling as he tried to stand still. He couldn't remember a time when he had felt his heartbeat so clearly. Court felt his legs start to buckle from under him and staggered backward until he slammed his back against his car. His legs finally gave out and he slid down the side of the vehicle until his butt hit the ground. He took in gasps of air as he stared up at the stars that were still visible despite the city's abundant light pollution.

Just as Court thought that matters couldn't get any worse, the ringing noise returned to his left ear. It was much quieter than it had been when it started in the lecture hall, but he heard it nonetheless. He shook his head in anguish as the sound moved to his right ear as well. In reaction to the unpleasant sensation filling his mind, he lowered his head and did his best to cover it with his arms. The ringing started to increase in volume as it had before, but this time did so much more gradually. He pressed his hands even tighter against his ears, in a futile effort to drown out the ringing that had seeped its way inside his head.

Court began to rock himself back and forth as he sat on the ground. His thoughts were quickly drowned out by the unbearable noise. Finally, not being able to handle the sound anymore, he stumbled to his feet. He screamed and shook his head like a madman as he ran circles around his vehicle. When the noise persisted, he lightly hit his forehead against the roof of his car. He continued to smack his face against his vehicle as the ringing grew higher in pitch. The more pain the noise caused, the harder he slammed his head against his car to try to draw focus away from his ears.

After several minutes of the strange scene, the ringing suddenly ceased. He stood there staring at the top of his car, breathing heavily. As more of his rational thinking returned, he noticed the stinging pain coming from his forehead. He brought his fingers up and lightly touched the area that hurt the most. Court brought his hand down to where he could see it in the dim light of the residential streetlamps and spotted a liquid on his fingers that he immediately identified as blood. He stood there, unable to comprehend the fact that he had slammed his head against his car so much that he had caused it to bleed.

Court was frozen in shock for several seconds until he faintly began to giggle. This gradually started to turn into a chuckle, which quickly escalated to light laughter from there. The strange events of the day had finally gotten to him and his mind just snapped. He couldn't help but laugh at the strangeness of the situation he was in, because he didn't know what else to do. Slowly, he climbed into his car and shut the door while still laughing to himself. His laughter grew into full-blown cackling that filled the vehicle. Very quickly his sides began to hurt, but despite this, he continued to laugh as a small trickle of blood moved down the middle of his face.

Matt felt the sweat building on his fingertips but he wouldn't let that stop him from typing. His tolerance for the number stations had improved dramatically and he wasn't going to let it go to waste. He felt a bubbling sense of accomplishment as he made his way through another series of integers. It had been roughly forty minutes since he had started writing things down and he was finally finding a rhythm, something he hadn't been able to accomplish before. He honestly thought there was a good chance that he might be able to stick with it until the last number was read. Suddenly, the front door flew open and he turned to see Court fly into the apartment with a look of rage on his face.

"You son of a bitch!" Court screamed.

"W-where have you been?" Matt asked in his best attempt to fake concern.

"Sleeping in my car!" Court yelled as he crossed the living room, "I couldn't make it home last night because this horrible ringing noise in my ears caused me to pass out." He stopped a good ten feet from his roommate and pointed at him, "It's the same kind of ringing that you told me you were having problems with last week!"

Matt slowly took off his headphones and gently placed them on the desk. He swallowed a bit of his saliva as he asked, "Did you see them?"

That question was enough to set Court off and he charged forward. Before Matt could react, Court had grabbed hold of his shirt collar and pulled him from his seat. He stared directly into his roommate's eyes with a burning rage. "You don't give a crap about me, do you?!" he screamed a second before throwing Matt to the floor.

"Of course I do," Matt whimpered as he shrunk into a ball. "I just wanted to know if you had seen the shadows yet."

Court stepped over his roommate and growled, "Why would that matter?"

"Well, uh...it would be...they can be...dangerous," Matt stammered.

"Oh they're dangerous, are they?" Court screamed as he bent down toward his former friend's face, "And here

I thought they were so friendly from my experience with the one that chased me through the library last night."

"So you have seen them," Matt smiled. "You understand me now."

Court grabbed ahold of his collar and pulled him up so he was closer to him. "I still don't understand why you're acting like a freak," he whispered. "All I know is that there is something after me, and you're the only person I know of that has seen it." He got right in Matt's face and growled, "What is it?"

"I-It's a shadow," came the whimpered reply.

Court slammed his roommate against the floor and then pulled him back up. "I'm gonna need more than that, you asshat!"

"I don't know anything else!" Matt cried just before he was slammed against the floor again.

"I know you know more than you're telling me!" Court screamed, "Who are they? What do they want? Why are they after me?"

Matt buckled under the onslaught of questions and cried out, "It's because you've heard the numbers!"

"What? Are you talking about the few seconds I heard last week? They're after me because of that?" Court asked. He thought about it for a moment then added, "I didn't see any of those things until yesterday. Why would they wait a whole week before coming after me?" He stared at his roommate. "Why me? I've only heard a few seconds of it." That's when he noticed a look on Matt's face that made it all too clear that he was hiding something. Court balled his fists together as he asked, "What did you do?"

"N-nothing, I-I swear," Matt whimpered as he shook like a leaf caught in the wind.

"What did you do!" Court roared.

"I've been unplugging my headphones at night," Matt admitted. "The radio turns to number stations by itself. I-I knew you would be susceptible to the transmissions if you were asleep."

"Why would you do that!" Court screamed as he threw a punch that hit his roommate square in the nose.

Matt cupped his hands over his injured appendage as he felt the sensations of blood trickling toward the back of his nasal cavities. "There was no other way," Matt started to say before he had to stop and swallow a bit of blood. "It was the only way you would understand what I've been going through."

"I never wanted to understand!" Court shrieked as he kicked Matt in the stomach.

Matt tried to scramble away from the onslaught, but he was too slow. Court grabbed ahold of his roommate and delivered a series of blows to his stomach. Matt kicked with his bare feet and managed to knock his attacker back a bit. He flipped onto his hurting stomach and tried to get up, but Court tackled him to the floor. Court took his left elbow and drove it into Matt's lower back to inflict as much pain as possible. The pinned man cried out for mercy, but none was given as blow after blow continued to be delivered into his back.

"They won't stop!" Matt screamed.

Court hesitated for a moment, then brought his elbow down again. He ground it in just below his roommate's shoulder blade as he asked, "What was that?"

"The shadows," Matt gasped out. "They won't stop coming after you now that you've heard the numbers enough to draw them to you."

Court grabbed ahold of Matt's side and flipped him over so he could look at his face. "How have you been able to keep them from getting to you? You never leave this damn apartment!"

"I found a way to keep them at bay," Matt quickly spat out a second prior to coughing up a bit of blood.

"Tell me!" Court growled as he brought his fist back to intimidate his roommate.

"It's the numbers!" Matt flinched from the fear of being punched again. "They want us to solve the secret of the numbers."

"Why?"

"I don't know," Matt admitted, "but what I do know is that it keeps them from coming for me. The more you listen to the number stations, the less the shadows show up. And...and the ringing noise starts to go away a-after a while."

Court took a few steps back from the carnage and looked toward the setup on his roommate's desk. He stared at the radio as a dozen thoughts raced through his mind. Matt groaned as he stumbled to his feet and took a few timid steps toward his unhappy friend.

"It's the only way," Matt said as he placed a hand on Court's shoulder. "You have to help me solve the mystery of the numbers."

"Don't touch me!" Court yelled as he slapped Matt's hand away. He looked his former friend dead in the eyes as he said, "You listen to me, because I'm only going to say this once. I'll help you with this." Upon noticing a smile on Matt's face, he quickly added, "I'll help you because it might be the only thing that keeps those...those things away from me." He shoved his roommate back. "But as far as you and me are concerned, we're done. As soon as we figure this out, you're gone. I never want to see your face again."

With that, Court headed to his bedroom, slamming his door behind him. Matt was left all alone in the silence, slowly realizing that he had permanently destroyed a friendship.

Part 4

Mysteries Resolved and Unresolved

Court sat in one of the uncomfortable chairs the University had provided for the apartment while looking at his phone with his music at full blast. The headphones were adequate to drown out the sound of whatever number station Matt was carefully listening to. Every once and a while, he would look up to see how things were going. His former friend was always quickly typing out integers on the computer without any signs of slowing down. He was honestly impressed by the amount of diligence that Matt put into it. His roommate would sit there for hours doing nothing else but typing whatever numbers were spewed out from the random voice crackling over the radio.

Suddenly, Court's music was interrupted by an incoming call from Madison. He let out a deep sigh and then stood up and hurried into his bedroom. He shut his door while answering, "What is it?"

"I called to check in on you," Madison replied.

"You haven't called to see how Matt is doing?"

"No," Madison sharply responded. There was a pause and then she continued, "He hasn't answered any of my calls. Not to mention, he tried to attack me when I stopped by the other day."

"He did what?" Court sputtered out in shock.

"I guess he didn't tell you," Madison sighed. "I came to visit him a few days ago when you weren't at your place. He started acting really aggressive and it was honestly scary as hell. I was going to leave but he tried to force me not to. I had to kick him just to get away."

"Jesus, I..." Court shook his head in disgust, "I had no idea," he sighed. "I'm really sorry that happened. He shouldn't have done that."

"I know," Madison sharply replied with a hint of annoyance, "that's why I'm checking up on you. Matt isn't in the right state of mind. He's dangerous. I wanted to make sure that he hadn't hurt you or himself."

"Don't worry, he hasn't hurt me," Court replied. "He hasn't done anything to hurt himself either."

Madison let out a sigh of relief before asking, "How is he doing? Does it seem like he's starting to at least try to act normal?"

"No," Court solemnly answered, "if anything, it's getting worse. He hasn't left the apartment in days. Plus, almost all his time is devoted to typing everything he hears over the radio."

"We need to get him help," Madison strongly insisted. "If he's getting worse, he needs a professional. We're past the point where just being good friends and giving him space will fix the problem. I've got the number of a mental health clinic that I found. We can call and have someone there to pick him up in less than an hour."

"No!" Court yelled. He immediately realized how suspicious that must have sounded and shifted his tone to sound calm. "No, we can't do that. It's probably really expensive to put him in there. Among the three of us, we barely have money to pay for our classes, let alone something like that."

"So what?" Madison scoffed in agitation. "You're going to let him mentally deteriorate just to keep him from getting hit with a huge bill?"

"He's not going to mentally deteriorate," Court said in a half chuckle to try to add some brevity to the situation. "He's been staying here with me the past few days and he hasn't hurt himself or done anything crazy." He took in a deep breath before going all in on his lie. "I'll level with you, I honestly think it's just stress."

"Stress?" Madison scoffed. "Stress from what?"

"That huge research paper he has to do," Court continued. "He has to make sure he puts something together that's good enough to get a passing grade from Professor Burrows. If he doesn't get it right, he has to stay an additional semester. That would throw a wrench in his plans. Plus, that paper's gonna end up being well over a hundred pages. That's a lot to churn out in just one semester."

"Sure," Madison skeptically replied. She thought for a moment and said, "Even if it is just stress, he shouldn't spend all his time in the same place. A change in scenery would probably be really good for him. I think it might be a good idea if he stays with me for a few days."

A rush of anxiety fluttered through Court as he thought about the shadows and what they would do to Matt, or even worse, him, if either of them were away from the stations for that long. "No," Court bluntly replied, "he's doing fine here with me."

"You don't think it's a bad idea to keep him around the thing that he's obsessing over?" Madison grew a little frustrated. "Come on Court, the only thing he could talk about when I saw him last was the numbers. It's not healthy for him. He needs to go somewhere else."

"No, he doesn't," Court snapped. "I think this conversation is over."

Before Madison could object, Court ended the call. A twinge of guilt hit his stomach, but he quickly shook it off as he opened his door and shuffled back into the living room where Matt was still furiously typing away. He walked up behind him and listened to the female voice as she spat out random numbers over the airwaves.

"Who was that?" Matt asked with an emotionless tone.

"It was Madison," Court replied. "She wanted to see how you and I were doing. I told her we were fine, but...she insisted that you should stay with her for a few days. She thought it would be good for your mental health."

"What did you tell her?" Matt asked as he continued to type.

"I said that wasn't necessary and ended the call."

"Good," Matt nodded. "Are you ready to trade spots?" he asked.

"I'm ready when you are," Court reluctantly replied as he let out a deep sigh.

As fluidly as possible, Matt got out of the chair and moved off to his left. The second he had left the seat, Court sat down and typed out the last two integers that had been called out then caught back up with the voice over the radio. Matt moved into the kitchen, leaving Court to type out the numbers. Court let out a deep but quiet groan as he wondered how long he would be able to hold out this time before the ringing became too much to handle.

Madison looked up from her phone as the office door swung open and Detective Robison stepped out. She smiled as she stuck her phone in her pocket and stood up. Robison spotted her and wore a confused look for a few seconds until he registered who she was. He walked over and held out a hand for her to shake.

"It's good to see you, Maddy," Robison smiled.

"You too, Mr. Robison," she replied.

He chuckled, "You're an adult now, you don't have to call me by my last name. Just call me Tom."

"Well then," she clapped her hands together, "it's nice to see you again...Tom."

"What brings you to the station?" Tom asked. "You wanting to check out your dad's old stomping grounds?"

"Actually, I was hoping I could ask you for a favor."

"A favor?" Tom replied quizzically. He slowly added, "Well, I guess it depends on the favor." He pointed to his office, "Do you mind if we step inside?"

"Of course not," Madison said as she walked through the office doorway. She had a seat in one of the two chairs in front of the officer's desk.

Tom let out a loud sigh as he sat back down in his chair and scooted himself forward. "So," he began, "what are you needing from me today?"

"You still handle the cases over by the college, right?"

Tom nodded. "Last time I checked, yes." He leaned forward, "Why? Do you think something went down there?"

"Kind of," Madison said with some hesitation. She took in a deep breath and then quickly spit out, "I need you to help me get my boyfriend out of his apartment that's just off campus."

"Is this some sort of domestic dispute?" Tom asked. He lowered his voice as he continued, "Did he hurt you?"

"No!" Madison quickly responded. "It wasn't anything like that. It's just...I'm scared that he might hurt himself."

"So he's suicidal," Tom said as he leaned back in his chair.

"No, well...not exactly, he's had a mental breakdown. He suddenly became obsessed with number stations. Do you know what those are?" Tom shook his head so she started to explain, "They're radio stations where people do nothing but read off random numbers for hours at a time." Madison looked Tom in the eyes as she continued, "My boyfriend believes that there's some hidden meaning in the numbers and that he has to solve it. He's been locked in his apartment for well over a week doing nothing else but listening to his radio."

"So, your man has gone crazy," Tom muttered to himself. He took a moment to absorb what Madison had said, and then he crossed his arms and let out a slow sigh. "Maddy," he hesitated before inquiring, "has a crime been committed at the apartment?"

"No," she replied, "but I'm concerned for his well-being. He has a roommate, and I'm scared he might do a lot more than just hurt himself."

"That's all well and good," Tom said as he gently placed a hand on his desk, "but if a crime hasn't occurred on the property, I can't help you."

"But...I just told you that he might hurt someone," Madison protested.

"I get that," Tom nodded while keeping a calm voice, "but my job is to catch people who have committed a crime. I don't get called in to solve murders that people think are going to happen. Something actually has to happen first."

"So you can't help me," Madison said in a defeated tone.

"I'm sorry Maddy," Tom shook his head. "I really am. I wish I could do something, but my hands are tied." He looked her in the eyes. "The best thing you can do for your man is convince him that he needs to get help. Outside of that, there's nothing I can do until he does something illegal."

Madison shook her head in disappointment and stood up. "Whatever," she solemnly said as she went to leave.

"Maddy!" Tom hollered to stop her. He waited for her to turn around before saying, "The second anything happens you call me, okay?" Tom stood up, walked around the desk and hugged Madison. "I'll have the entire department down there in a heartbeat. Take care of yourself, Maddy."

"I will, Tom," she said as she let go and turned to leave the office.

"Be careful," Tom said quickly. He made a mental note to get with his superior to discuss what Maddy had told him while silently hoping his gut feeling about the situation was completely wrong.

Madison simply nodded at him before exiting the room. She quickly moved down the hallway of the police precinct, feeling hurt at the fact that Tom wouldn't help her. Even though she was thoroughly disappointed with her meeting, she tried her best not to show it. Once she made it out to her car and got in, she started to bang her palms against the steering wheel in complete frustration. Matt was getting worse, and it seemed like no one cared except her. First Court didn't want to help, and now Detective Robison couldn't. She let out a long breath to calm down. As she did, an idea began to form in her head. She sat there for a few minutes, just letting the plan form in her mind. When all the details had taken shape in her mind, Madison put her car in drive and headed out of the parking lot. If no one else was going to help, then she would do what needed to be done herself.

Matt shuffled into his bedroom and sat down on his bed. He brought his hand up to his right ear and then slowly took it away to find a smear of blood on his fingers. Though he had started to build up a resistance to the number stations, it was clear that he wasn't immune just yet. After listening for close to six hours, there were bound to be some nasty side effects. He was suddenly overcome with a dizzying sensation and quickly laid down on his bed to remedy it. The ringing noise ran through his ears, which swiftly led to intense pain inside his head. He took a deep breath and waited a few minutes for it to subside.

He hated to admit to it, but his frustrations were starting to get the better of him. Court had been working alongside him for the past few days, but it had become abundantly clear who would be doing most of the work. Matt had a much higher tolerance for the numbers, so he got stuck typing away for hours at a time. His roommate seemed to be only able to handle an hour or so at a time, leaving him to handle almost seventy-five percent of the work. This led to him having numerous headaches alongside other pains that were so intense that blood from an orifice seemed like a reprieve.

The ringing in his ears finally stopped and Matt let out an uneasy sigh of relief. He felt his eyes growing heavy and was about to drift off into a much-needed moment of sleep when he sensed something. His body tensed up as he distinctly felt someone staring at him. Gradually, he turned his head toward his door and was completely shocked to see a shadow standing there. He bolted out of his bed and stood in tense anticipation of what the ethereal being was there to do.

“What do you want?” he asked quietly. When the presence didn’t respond he yelled, “All I’ve been doing is typing out your damn numbers! I've done what you've asked. What more do you want from me!"

The shadow hissed, "She."

"She?" Matt repeated with a mix of confusion and surprise. The mysterious entities had never said anything else besides the word numbers. He was curious as to why that would change now. "What do you mean by 'she'?" He pondered before rephrasing the question, "Who is she?"

"She is coming," the shadow hissed. "Your she."

"Your she," Matt repeated several times to himself. "My she!" he suddenly exclaimed upon realizing what the presence meant. "You mean Madison!"

The ethereal being hissed, "She destroy."

Matt knew what the shadow meant but still asked, "She's coming to destroy? Destroy what?" The answer to his question dawned on him and he whispered, "My radio."

The strange entity simply replied with, "Stop her," before disappearing into thin air.

"Don't worry, I'll stop her," Matt whispered to himself.

"Are you okay?" Court asked as he walked into Matt's room.

"What are you doing in here?" Matt yelled. "What about the numbers!"

"The station cut out," Court snapped. "There's nothing more for me to write down." He glared at Matt, "What were you yelling about?"

"I'm frustrated," Matt replied. "All of this work, and we still haven't collected everything yet." He grumbled, "I think it's perfectly fine if I yell to myself about it."

"Sure." Court rolled his eyes as he walked out of the room.

Matt sat on his bed and let out a deep breath. Now he had to find something to occupy his mind while he waited for the arrival of his uninvited guest.

Madison tentatively opened the door, one painstaking inch at a time. She was incredibly thankful that the key Matt had given to her still worked. Carefully, she took a timid step into the dark apartment and waited for her eyes to adjust. As she began to scan the area around her, she was relieved to see that there was no one in the kitchen or living room. Gradually and slowly, she closed the door behind her, then started to tiptoe across the floor. She had to use all the strength in her legs to make sure that she stepped as lightly as possible.

After a few painstaking minutes, she was able to make it across the living room to Matt's desk. She noticed that the computer hadn't been turned off yet and went to investigate. Madison moved the mouse a bit and the screen lit up, causing her to be temporarily blinded. She blinked a few times as her eyes adjusted enough to where she was able to look at the screen. A wave of horror ran through her as she stared at the open document that was nothing more than a jumble of random integers. She looked to see how many pages there were and gasped when she saw the cursor was on page 489 of 490. It would have taken at least a week or two to type all that out. That's when she realized that Court had been lying to her. Matt was getting much worse, which meant she had to put a stop to things right away.

"Did you find what you were looking for?"

Madison whipped her head toward the entrance to Matt's side of the apartment to find him standing in near darkness. He took a step forward and the light from the computer screen illuminated his features. His hair was disgustingly greasy, and she could almost see the filth that covered his body. From where he was, she was already able to smell his foul body odor. The pungent stench assailed her nostrils and reminded her of the smell that normally came from a dumpster behind a fast-food place. It was clear he hadn't showered in several days, which meant he had been sitting in his own sweat and filth.

"I hope you found what you were looking for," Matt grinned as he took another step toward his desk.

Madison quickly stood up and when Matt took another step, she moved back from the desk. With the light from the computer, she could see the crazed look that was shining in his eyes.

"What's the matter, Madison?" Matt said, licking his lips. "You seem a little tense." He pretended to jump forward and she flinched in response. "Are you scared of me?" he chuckled.

"This has gone on long enough," Madison stammered.

"What has?" he inquired with a light chuckle.

"This madness!" she said pointing at the computer screen. "There's nothing hidden in the numbers. Just face it, you're going crazy and you need help."

Matt laughed, "Oh, that's where you're wrong." He shook his head, "The numbers mean so much. That's why the shadow people have been making sure I solve the mystery."

"There are no shadow people," Madison said in desperation. "Your mind is playing tricks on you."

"Court sees them," Matt smirked.

A new sense of fear ran through her as she looked over her shoulder toward where Court's room was. She finally understood why he had been so short with her a few days ago. Why he hadn't been returning any of her calls. He was going mad as well. Most likely he was after the same, insane goal that Matt was. Madison drew her gaze toward the radio, and in her mind, the source of all the madness that had overtaken two people who were very important to her. She knew if she broke that, the insanity would end.

"Why did you come here?" Matt asked, "I know it wasn't to check up on Court or me because it's almost three in the morning. So why are you here?"

"Because I'm genuinely concerned about you," Madison gently responded. "You're both not in the right state of mind. You need to get help."

"We don't need any help," Matt snapped. "We just need to be left to our work in peace."

"Then what?" Madison inquired. He didn't respond so she said, "You don't know, do you? That's because nothing will happen once you get them all. You'll still be in the same apartment, just you and Court, and nothing will have changed."

"You lie," Matt growled. "You don't know what you're talking about. You're just an obstacle that's blocking our way."

"That's not true." Madison pleaded, "I'm here to help you, but you need to let me. You have to let this all go and walk out that door with me." Madison slowly held out her hand for him to take.

Matt hesitated, then slowly, he started to raise his hand out to meet hers. Just before they touched, he pulled his hand back. "No!" he shouted. "You're just here to smash the radio! You only want to stop what I'm doing!"

He lunged toward Madison but was met with a kick to his right leg that caused him to stumble back. She moved to pick up the radio and smash it on the ground, successfully wrapping her fingers around it. Seeing her progress toward her goal sent an unbridled rage through him. He moved with incredible speed and reached her before she could fully raise the radio. Matt ripped back Madison's hands and the radio fell a few inches back onto the table with a thud. He pulled her toward him, and she brought her head back and delivered an imperfect headbutt.

Madison once again lunged for the radio, but he grabbed ahold of her before she made it. The rage pumping through him made the pain he was feeling from the headbutt seem insignificant. He took her head and slammed it against the desk. Matt let go of her and she fell to the floor while groaning in pain. He grabbed hold of her ankles and started to drag her away from the desk. She wildly kicked her legs and managed to get her left one free to deliver a hit to his face. He let go of her and she started to frantically crawl back toward the radio.

Matt's anger pushed him forward and he managed to grab Madison by the shoulders. He took his left hand and snatched ahold of her head. With the muscles in his arm flexing, he slammed Madison's face into the ground at full force. He felt her body go limp in his grasp and flipped her onto her back. In the moment, he could tell that she was still alive, but not for long. He wrapped his hands around her throat and started to squeeze. A look of desperation appeared in her eyes and she delivered a brutal knee to his groin. He let go and cried out in pain as Madison started to scramble away from him.

That was the last straw for Matt, and he jumped on top of her before she could get far. He grabbed hold of her head and squeezed with all his might, just to make sure it wasn't going anywhere. Then he slammed her skull into the floor as hard as he could. Madison gasped in agony as he picked her head back up and slammed it again. She desperately fought and kicked to break free, but his grip on her head wouldn't loosen. There was no letting up as he continued to bash her skull into the ground, well after the blood started to appear. He watched as the light in her eyes grew dim, continuing to pound the back of her head against the apartment floor until her struggling ceased. Finally, he let go of Madison's face and gasped as he fell back off the now-deceased body of his girlfriend.

"What have you done!" Court cried.

Matt looked up to see his roommate run over and kneel next to Madison's body. He took a deep breath as he stumbled to his feet and then told Court, "What had to be done. She was trying to destroy the radio."

"Shut up!" Court screamed. He leapt toward Matt and tackled him to the floor. Without any hesitation, he delivered a series of vicious blows to the murderer's face while his roommate simply sat there and took the punishment. "Screw you and your numbers!" he shouted as he stood up.

Matt lay on the floor coughing up some of the blood he had swallowed. Court had broken his nose and now blood was freely flowing down his face. "You know we have to finish it Court," he gasped in between coughs. "If we don't...they'll tear us to shreds." He weakly chuckled, "I had to do it. You know that."

"I hate you," Court growled as he looked down at Matt in absolute disgust. "With every fiber of my being, I want to squeeze the life out of you."

"But you won't," Matt grinned.

"Not yet," Court said kneeling to look Matt in the eyes with a gaze of pure hatred. He watched the smile fade from his accomplice's face then said, "When all these numbers are down, and those things finally leave us alone. Make no mistake, I will kill you." He grabbed the murderer by his shirt and pulled him close, "There's no way you make it out of this alive, Matt. Either those things tear you to shreds or I will."

Court felt his eyes starting to dry from all the time he had spent fixated on his computer screen. Of course, the smell of Madison's decaying body wasn't helping the situation either. Though it had only been three days since Matt had killed her, she was already showing the first signs of rot. He knew that in a few minutes, the ringing noise would sound in his ears, which was something he was tired of having to deal with. With a loud sigh, he tried to continue his efforts to type but quickly lost momentum. He finally pushed himself back from the computer and folded his arms.

"What are you doing!" Matt screamed as he ran over to him. "You need to keep typing out the numbers!"

"Screw this!" Court yelled. "I'm not doing this any longer." He turned the chair to face Matt, "We've been doing this for well over a week now, and it doesn't feel like we've put a dent in it." He pointed at the open document on the computer, "Over five hundred pages, and we're still not done! Doesn't that seem a little suspicious to you?"

"No," Matt said, "if it were so easy to unravel the mystery of the numbers, dozens of people would have done it by now. That's why it's so important we do it. We'll be the first. The only ones to truly understand the number stations. The shadow people are counting on us."

"Screw them," Court grumbled. "All they do is show up and look spooky. Why don't they do it themselves if it's so important?"

"Because they need us to," Matt insisted. "We have something they don't."

"What? We actually exist?"

Matt gasped, appalled as he pointed at his accomplice, "You know they exist. You've seen them."

Court stood up from the chair, "Well, now I'm not so sure. I think I was under a lot of stress when I saw them." He shrugged, "They're just figments of our imagination."

"Why are you doing this?" Matt asked as his eyes nervously darted around the room. "Why are you questioning them like this? You're only making things worse for us."

"How?" Court laughed, "They don't even exist!"

Matt noticed movement out of the corner of his eye and glanced toward his room to see a shadow standing just over ten feet from them. He looked the other way and saw another of the ethereal beings slowly moving forward. Filled with terror, he pivoted to look at the kitchen and saw a final one also drawing closer.

"They're here!" Matt cried out, "Apologize to them!"

"Oh god," Court whispered as he frantically glanced between the different shadows as they closed in.

The strange entities moved forward at a slow pace in such a way that it dragged out a single moment to where it seemed like an hour had passed. Fear rushed through Matt's body and he dropped down onto his knees. He bowed to show his reverence to the ethereal beings so they wouldn't harm him. Court shook his head and stubbornly stood his ground as they approached. This whole thing had gone on long enough. He had been a coward and had given in to the crazy delusions of his roommate. Now Madison was dead, all because he couldn't stand up to a simple shadow.

"I've had enough of this," Court said as he took a step forward.

The ethereal being that was coming directly at him suddenly teleported to where it was just a few inches from him. Court gasped as the shadow's hand reached out and grabbed his neck. He felt his windpipe constrict as the air was cut off from his lungs. The entity lifted him off the ground with ease and held him several inches in the air. Almost immediately, he felt lightheaded as the lack of oxygen was drawing him closer to unconsciousness. Just when he thought the end had come, the shadow let go of him and watched him fall to the floor. Court gasped and wheezed as he desperately tried to take in air.

The unnatural entity pointed at him. "Never again," it hissed.

"I'm so sorry for that," Matt groveled. "He's foolish. He'll never disrespect you again."

"Why are you doing this?" Court choked out.

"Numbers," the shadow on the left of him hissed.

"We've been writing down your damn numbers!" Court yelled. "They never end! We're never going to finish typing them."

"Close," the middle presence hissed. "Close to end."

The one on the right growled, "Don't stop."

In an instant, all three of the ethereal beings had vanished. Matt meticulously scanned the living room, looking to see if they truly were gone. Court continued to cough as he gently pressed on the area of his throat the shadow had grabbed hold of. There was no doubt in his mind it was going to bruise. Matt slowly climbed to his feet while his whole body trembled. He turned to his roommate and stared at him before delivering a kick to his accomplice's side.

"What the hell!" Court yelled.

"You idiot!" Matt screamed. "You almost got us killed!" He leaned down and whispered, "They could have torn us to pieces, but they didn't. They showed us mercy." He stood back up, "It won't happen again."

Matt sat down at the computer and slightly turned the volume up on the radio. Court remained on the ground as he tried to recover from what had just happened to him. He stared at his accomplice's back as he typed out the numbers that were being called out. After a few minutes, he finally got to his feet.

"Why do you keep doing this?" he asked.

Without stopping Matt replied, "Because it is fate that I solve this." He paused, then said, "The next part is up to you. Do you wish to help me, or end up a nameless corpse in the morgue?"

Court stood there in silence as he watched Matt type away. Finally, he replied to the question. "I'm not going to be a corpse." He leaned in to whisper, "I'll make sure of that."

Matt typed in the number he heard called out and waited for the next one. He sat there for several seconds before realizing that there wasn't going to be another one. "Oh my god!" he shouted in excitement.

"What?" Court asked as he ran out of his room.

"We've done it!" Matt shouted, "We've collected all the numbers!"

"Really?" Court said trying to sound excited. He quietly crept into the kitchen and cautiously took the butcher's knife out of the cutting block.

"Yeah, I just typed the last one that was read out. They haven't said anymore, so it has to be the last one."

"What do we do now?" Court asked as he slowly approached Matt with the knife behind his back.

"I-I don't know," Matt truthfully replied. He started scrolling through the document that contained all the collected data, looking for some clue, "The shadows didn't tell me what to do next."

"Maybe that's all we have to do," Court suggested as he prepared himself for what he was about to do.

"No, that can't be!" Matt said as he continued to scroll through the document, "Nothing has happened yet! Something has to happen!"

He moved his chair back a bit to get up, not realizing Court was right behind him. A split second before he was about to stand, he felt a sharp pain in his shoulder. Matt slowly looked over to see a large knife sticking out of it. He turned his gaze upward from the blade to see his former friend holding on to the weapon. He let out a whimpering gasp of agony as his attacker slowly pulled the blade out. Court grabbed Matt by his wounded shoulder and drove his thumb into the cut. The injured man screamed out in agony as his face was slammed into his computer's keyboard. Another stab was delivered, driving the knife into the top, right part of Matt's back.

"Why are you doing this?" Matt cried out.

"I told you," Court growled as he forcefully pulled his former accomplice up to a sitting position, "either way you weren't going to make it out alive. The shadows didn't kill you, so now I have to."

"Please don't do this."

"Why shouldn't I?" Court screamed. "You didn't show Madison any mercy when you bashed her brains out! I'm going to give you the same courtesy. I'll make sure you suffer."

Matt reached out his left hand which was covered in his blood and touched the screen with his trembling hand. He let his fingertips slide down the smooth surface as he gasped in pain. "But I finally got to see all the numbers," he gasped through the agony.

"And now you know you were wrong!" Court laughed. "Nothing happened! They didn't mean anything!"

Suddenly, a loud humming noise started to come from the computer. Court was distracted enough by the sound to bring his focus to the monitor where he noticed the screen glowing brighter. The volume on the radio suddenly came on at full blast as static started to sound off. The noises were loud enough that he was starting to feel a bit of pain in his ears. He stumbled back, away from Matt while trying to plug up his exposed appendages. His dying accomplice raised his head to see the computer screen shining at an intensity that was far beyond what it should have been able to. He started to laugh uncontrollably as the numbers on the document began to flash over the rest of the screen. Meanwhile, the pain became too intense for Court, and the knife fell from his hand as he dropped to his knees.

"What the hell is happening!" Court screamed.

"It needed blood!" Matt yelled in realization. "That's why it wasn't doing anything. It needs blood to start the process!" He continued to watch the data dance across the monitor while he whispered to himself, "It's so beautiful!"

The screen continued to engulf the room in an ever-increasing light while the radio grew in volume. Court screamed in pain as he grasped the sides of his head, reaching a level of agony that he had never experienced. The computer finally grew so bright that not a single thing in the room could be seen. The sounds of static had now ceased to make way for the screams of agony that came from the two doomed men. Screaming continued for several minutes until it suddenly ceased. The monitor burst into flames a few seconds later, returning the lighting in the room to how it had been before the unnatural incident. The room now lay empty. There were no signs of Matt and Court.

Robison walked through the door to all the commotion from dozens of people running around the crime scene. The chaos of it all was the first thing he noticed, with the smell being the second. A familiar stench of rotting flesh filled the air, and made breathing through the nose impossible. He shook his head as he moved toward the medical examiner who was currently inspecting the deceased. After only a few steps, he was stopped by the first officer on the scene.

"Detective Robison," the officer held out his hand, "I'm Charles Murphy."

Robison shook his hand while asking, "So what the hell do we have here?"

Murphy gave a small cough, "The lady living at the apartment directly below called in saying she heard a lot of yelling. She said it seemed like someone was in a lot of pain. She also mentioned that there was a bright light coming through her ceiling."

"A bright light?" Robison repeated in confusion.

"Yeah, something strong enough that it was shining through the floorboards into her apartment."

Robison examined the floor, "It would take a lot of light to get through." He had a bad feeling in the pit of his stomach. This whole scene was starting to seem a little too familiar.

"Anyways," Murphy paused to scan his notes, "I was the one who was sent out. When I arrived, no one answered the door. I was going to leave when I smelt it." He gestured toward the body, "I knew that smell anywhere, so there was no doubt in my mind that something was wrong. I broke in the door and that's when I found her."

Robison nodded, "Does she rent the apartment?"

Murphy shook his head, "A Courtland Jacobs and Matthew Sampson do. They're students at Southridge."

A terrible feeling hit Robison directly in the gut. Even before he moved to examine the crime scene the pieces were starting to form. He pushed by Murphy and made a beeline for the medical examiner. His gut was turning over as his heart beat faster. He didn't want to look down at the body because he knew who it might be, but he had to. Slowly, he let his eyes start on the victim's shoes. He had seen them a week ago in his office. From that small image alone, he already knew who it was, but he still forced himself to move his eyes up the body toward the head, to the decomposing face of Madison Daniels.

"You doing okay detective?" the medical examiner asked.

Robison ignored the question as he lowered himself to the ground. He reached out to touch her but stopped himself. The last thing he wanted to do was contaminate a crime scene. He stared at her bloating face and tried his hardest to hold back the tears.

"I'm so sorry Maddy," he whispered. "I didn't know it was this bad. I would have broken every protocol in the book to keep this from happening." He choked back a few tears. "This never should have happened. Especially, to you."

"Did you know her?" the medical examiner asked.

"Yeah," Robison replied quietly, "she was the daughter of my former partner. I've known her since she was five years old." He stood up and looked at all the manpower surrounding him. Robison shouted, "Do we have any leads on a killer?"

The commotion in the room ceased. Everyone froze and looked at Robison in silence. It was clear that no one had anything for him.

"Let me get this straight," Robison yelled, "we've got at least ten trained officers looking over a single apartment for several hours, and you mean to tell me that none of you have found a damn thing on our killers?" He felt his anger bubble up and screamed, "This is unacceptable! I want everyone in here to double their efforts! Now move your asses!"

Robison watched as everyone close to him scrambled around each other to put something together before he could reem them on an individual basis. He sighed, then finally did a quick scan of the room himself. After a long look, his eyes came to rest on the desk sitting against the back wall. He approached it and first noticed the computer that had been burnt to a crisp. Robison took note that the area around the computer wasn't singed in any way. That fact alone gave him a troubling sensation that made the hairs on the back of his neck stand up.

He moved his attention to the only other item on the desk that was burnt. It had been so severely damaged by whatever fire had gotten to it, that it took him a few moments of staring to even realize it was a radio. Robison crawled under the piece of furniture to check to see if the radio's power cord was plugged in. Upon finding that it was, he knew exactly what was going on. He crawled out from under the desk and lifted the radio just a bit to see that the material underneath it was completely unscathed.

"They actually did it," he whispered to himself. "They wrote down all the numbers." He shook his head, "Those poor bastards." He turned back toward the rest of the room and loudly announced, "All right people, it looks like we are not dealing with a normal homicide. We have a 983 on our hands." A round of murmuring filled the room, so Robison had to shout to be heard, "That means we're packing up everything and getting out of here. I'll be sure to put together the report, so the rest of you can get out."

"Jesus, I didn't even think it existed," the medical examiner said as he packed up his things.

"Officially they don't," Robison replied, "I've only seen one before now." He shook his head, "But once you see one, you can never forget it."

"Well, good luck with the report," the examiner said as he moved toward the door.

"Thanks," Robison yelled after him.

He waited for the room to clear out before kneeling next to Madison's body. "Looks like I know what happened to your killers," he said solemnly. "I can't believe I'm saying this, but they got far worse than they deserved." He shuddered as he stood up, "You didn't deserve what happened to you. But they didn't deserve what happened to them either."

Robison walked to the front door and slowly opened it. He took a look over his shoulder at the tainted apartment. The place would never be safe for anyone to live in. He would hate to be the person to tell everyone else in the building that they had to move. That's why he wouldn't be doing it. He would get a few of the grunts in his department to seal off the area and deliver the bad news. Robison shook his head as he shut the door behind him. Some things have to be contained at all costs, and what happened in that apartment was one of them.

Radar DeBoard is just a simple horror writer, living in the bleak state of Kansas. Recently, he has grown weary of the limitations of his craft when it comes to scares. Sure, he has terrified many thanks to having four published books to his name as well as being featured in dozens of horror anthologies, but the fear from those stories wears off. He wishes to create something so horrific that it lingers in the reader's mind for years to come. Creating something of such unfathomable terror would cement him in the brains of those who purchase his books. Plus, it would be like he left a piece of himself in each copy of his work. A small bit of himself that can grow and watch, waiting for the right time to deliver a final fright.

Made in the USA
Columbia, SC
16 September 2024

41811188R00068